A New Boyfriend . . .
or a New Problem?

"Come watch us college guys play basketball, and then we can spend the rest of the day together," Toby Jackson said. He had just driven DeeDee home from their first date. They were sitting in his car, parked in front of the Smith home.

"That sounds nice," DeeDee said softly, studying Toby from under her lashes.

"Just nice?" Toby asked, sliding a little closer to her.

"More than nice," DeeDee answered. Her heart was beating rapidly as his face bent toward hers. DeeDee closed her eyes and felt the softest, sweetest sensation as his lips brushed over hers. Then Toby gathered her in his arms and pressed her against him.

DeeDee's head was spinning. Things were moving fast with Toby, but she didn't have the slightest desire to slow them down.

Books in the RIVER HEIGHTS ™ Series

Available from ARCHWAY Paperbacks

River HEIGHTS™ #13

A MIND OF HER OWN

CAROLYN KEENE

AN ARCHWAY PAPERBACK
Published by POCKET BOOKS

New York London Toronto Sydney Tokyo Singapore

AN ARCHWAY PAPERBACK *Original*

An Archway Paperback published by
POCKET BOOKS, a division of Simon & Schuster Inc.
1230 Avenue of the Americas, New York, NY 10020

Copyright © 1991 by Simon & Schuster Inc.
Produced by Mega-Books of New York, Inc.

ISBN: 0-671-73117-3

First Archway Paperback printing November 1991

10 9 8 7 6 5 4 3 2 1

AN ARCHWAY PAPERBACK and colophon are registered trademarks of Simon & Schuster Inc.

RIVER HEIGHTS is a trademark of Simon & Schuster Inc.

Cover art by Carla Sormanti

Printed in the U.S.A.

IL 6+

A MIND OF HER OWN

1

"Well, well, well," said Robin Fisher on Monday morning. "If it isn't the Incredible Vanishing Woman." Robin, tall and slim with short dark brown hair, was wearing a puffy, bright orange down jacket and hot pink stirrup pants. Her large brown eyes were fixed accusingly on Lacey Dupree in the student parking lot of River Heights High School.

Lacey Dupree, after climbing out of her beat-up yellow Buick, met Robin's angry gaze nervously. Lacey knew why Robin was upset. She also knew she'd have to face Robin then or risk losing her friendship forever.

Swallowing past the lump that had formed in her throat, Lacey locked her car and trudged across the parking lot. At the same moment Lacey's other best friend, Nikki Masters, pulled her metallic blue Camaro into the lot, parked near Robin, and got out. Nikki's light blond hair gleamed in the late-winter sunlight, and her slender figure looked great in a powder blue wool coat.

Lacey approached her friends and smiled apologetically. "Go ahead," she said. "Yell at me. I guess I deserve it."

"Yell at you?" Robin demanded, her voice rising. "Why on earth would I want to yell at you? Just because you ditched me on one of the most important nights of my life? Or maybe because you've suddenly undergone a major personality change and don't care about your friends anymore? Gee, Lacey, I don't know what you're talking about!"

"I haven't changed—" Lacey began, but Robin cut her off.

"Oh, no? Then maybe you can explain your new wardrobe." Robin pointed at Lacey's outfit.

Lacey glanced down at her black leather jacket slashed with silver zippers, her black jeans, and her black cowboy boots. Lacey's new boyfriend, Tom Stratton, had just given her the jacket, one of his old ones. She'd bought the jeans at the River Heights Mall and found the cowboy boots in the back of her closet. Her fluffy red hair, usually subdued in a braid, was hanging loose in cloud-like waves around her face.

"Well, maybe I *am* dressing a little differently," Lacey admitted, "but——"

"But nothing," Robin interrupted again. "You *have* changed. You used to be a friend we could count on, but not anymore. Not after you didn't come to see me win second place in the talent show on Friday night. You knew——"

"Come on, Robin," Nikki said. "Give Lacey a chance to explain."

"I don't know why *you're* being so understanding," Robin said to Nikki. "You and Tim won *first* place, and Lacey wasn't there to watch you, either. And she also stood up her own boyfriend. Rick sat all by himself."

"I can explain, if you'll just give me a chance," Lacey tried again.

"Don't bother," Robin said. "I know exactly where you were. With Tom Stratton, right?"

There was no point denying it. Lacey knew she had to tell her friends sooner or later that she had started dating Tom, Rick's older brother.

Rick had been Lacey's boyfriend, but while he had been in the hospital recuperating from a rock-climbing accident, he'd fallen for Katie Fox, a promising swimmer from another high school who had also suffered a sports injury. Then Lacey got to know Rick's brother, Tom, a senior at River Heights High. Tom was a part-time mechanic and an aspiring rock musician. Though Lacey and Tom couldn't have been more different, they were fast falling in love.

"I *was* with Tom," Lacey admitted, "and I'm sorry I couldn't cheer you guys on. But I needed some support myself Friday night. I caught Rick kissing Katie Fox in his back-yard, right before the talent show!"

"You're kidding!" Nikki said. "Oh, Lacey, I'm so sorry!"

"Maybe if you hadn't been running around behind Rick's back, he wouldn't have had to kiss Katie," Robin snapped.

"That's not fair," Lacey said, tears filling her light blue eyes. "Rick's the one who cheated on me. Why are you taking his side?"

"Because he hasn't become Dr. Jekyll and Mr. Hyde. He showed up for the talent show, without this Katie Fox, by the way. He's still someone I can trust."

"You don't believe me?" Lacey asked, a tear trickling down her freckled cheek.

"If you really want to know—*no!*" Robin grabbed her bookbag off the hood of Nikki's car and stormed off toward the school.

* * *

Earlier that morning DeeDee Smith had awakened with a start, her heart beating furiously.

Sitting straight up in bed, DeeDee rubbed her eyes and looked around her room. Her electronic typewriter sat on her desk, almost buried beneath stacks of the River Heights High *Record*. DeeDee, a senior, was editor in chief of the high school paper and rarely stopped thinking about it, even when she was home.

But right then her mind was on something else. That day was the day she could hear whether she'd been accepted to Kingston University. She'd applied for a special Early Acceptance, which meant she'd get a reply earlier than most.

DeeDee quickly showered, dressed, and started on her makeup. All her friends told her she was pretty, with her smooth brown skin, dark, serious eyes, and long, curly black hair. All DeeDee saw that day was a girl whose life might be over when the mail arrived. After hastily applying lip gloss and mascara, DeeDee grabbed her books and ran downstairs to the kitchen.

"Is that my little tiger?" asked Harold Smith, DeeDee's father, smiling at her over his cup of coffee. The tiger was the Kingston University mascot. Mr. Smith had attended

Kingston, and it was his dream to have DeeDee go there, too.

"I'm not a tiger yet," DeeDee said nervously, entering the kitchen and kissing her father on top of his bald head. A heavyset man in his forties, Harold Smith was an editor at the River Heights *News*.

"I'm sure something will show up in the mail this week, sweetheart," said Doreen Smith, DeeDee's mother. A slender, attractive woman, she worked part time at a daycare center.

"Well, when that acceptance shows up, I'm going to take you ladies out for a big celebration," Mr. Smith said. "I'll take you to Le Saint-Tropez or any restaurant you want. Price will be no object. It's not every day a man finds out his little girl is going to attend his alma mater."

"It *has* happened once already," DeeDee pointed out. DeeDee's older sister, Carol, was a sophomore at Kingston. "And you shouldn't just assume I'll get in. You might jinx me."

"There's a nice fat acceptance envelope from Kingston heading your way," Mr. Smith said, "and nothing we say or do now will stop it from getting here."

"I hope so," DeeDee mumbled as she poured milk over her cereal.

"I *know* so," Mr. Smith said confidently. "Kingston will be lucky to have you."

DeeDee wanted to cover her ears with her hands because the more her father talked about Kingston, the more panicky she felt. What if she didn't get in?

Almost worse, what if she did? DeeDee's father had always expected her to follow in his footsteps, first to Kingston and then on to become an editor at a newspaper. It had been easy for DeeDee to agree to this when her future had seemed so far away. Now, though, the future was almost here, and DeeDee wasn't sure if she wanted what her father wanted. But there was no way she could tell him that.

Brittany Tate stepped off the schoolbus in front of River Heights High School. She quickly spotted her two best friends, Kim Bishop and Samantha Daley, standing on the marble front steps of the north wing scanning the crowd in the quad.

Kim, blond and trim, was swiveling her head from side to side, her pointy nose high in the air. Samantha, a transplanted southern belle, delicately pretty with wide, cinnamon brown eyes that perfectly matched her permed brown hair, was also searching the crowd.

Brittany knew they were looking for her because she'd refused to talk to them all weekend. Kim and Samantha knew something was up, and they would corner her the first chance they got.

Brittany briefly considered trying to hide, then decided it might be more fun to make them beg for information. Tossing her glossy dark hair back, Brittany strode across the quad toward them.

"There you are!" Kim Bishop exclaimed, moving down the stairs toward Brittany. "So, where did you disappear to after the show?"

Kim had done a dance routine in the talent show and bombed, mainly because she hadn't practiced. Basically, though, she was a very talented dancer.

"I'm really sorry I couldn't be with you in your hour of need," Brittany said sweetly. "It must have hurt to be beaten by *Robin Fisher.* I mean, she's not even a real dancer, like you. She's a swimmer, for heaven's sake!"

Kim winced, and Brittany felt guilty for being so mean.

"That's not the worst part," Kim said. "Jeremy's not talking to me now. He said he was personally humiliated by my performance. Can you believe how self-centered he is? He's acting as if *he* was the one up on that stage." Kim's boyfriend, Jeremy Pratt, was known in the school as the King of Snobs. His parents were very rich and bought him everything he ever wanted, including a Porsche, which he never stopped bragging about.

"He's a jerk," Brittany said, nodding.

"You still haven't answered our question," Samantha drawled. "What happened to you Friday night after the show? And why wouldn't you talk to us all weekend?"

"You'll never believe this," Brittany said. She paused for dramatic effect. "Someone is trying to *blackmail* me."

Kim became instantly alert. Samantha, too, pushed closer to Brittany, eager to hear every word.

Brittany checked over her shoulder to make sure no one else was near enough to hear. "Remember Nikki and Tim's act in the show?" she began.

"How could I forget?" Kim asked, rolling her eyes. "All that applause is still ringing in my ears!"

Nikki and Tim had performed a love scene from a play called *The Blue Moon Luncheonette*, in which two lovers, Rita and Lamont, made up after a big fight.

"Well, you remember the big bucket of water Nikki threw at Tim at the end of the scene?" Brittany asked.

"That was great," Samantha said enthusiastically. "I couldn't believe she actually dumped real water on him. It made the whole scene."

"Nikki was *supposed* to throw a plate of spaghetti at him, but I dumped it in my purse right before the scene," Brittany said.

"Ewww!" Kim said. "Why did you do that?"

Brittany sighed. "Because I was trying to wreck their scene, of course! I was trying to leave them without an ending for the scene. It was just bad luck that Nikki thought fast and threw the water instead. Sometimes I hate that girl."

Hate was hardly strong enough to describe how Brittany really felt about Nikki Masters. Nikki, Brittany thought, was the cause of all her problems. Beautiful, blond Nikki with her rich parents and gorgeous boyfriend, Tim Cooper. Brittany had spent weeks trying to get Tim away from Nikki, but Tim hadn't fallen. And if being rich and having a beautiful boyfriend wasn't bad enough, Nikki's great-grandfather had *founded* the River Heights Country Club. The very club Brittany had had to work two jobs to earn the money to join. Everything was handed to Nikki on a silver platter. To Brittany it wasn't fair.

Just once Brittany had wanted to get the

best of that girl. Brittany thought stealing the spaghetti would have been the perfect plan, but it had all blown up in her face.

"So what does blackmail have to do with this?" Kim asked, her blue eyes narrowing.

Brittany leaned in closer to her friends. "Someone saw me steal the spaghetti," she told them in a low voice. "And the person sent me a note telling me to meet him at Slim and Shorty's Cafe after the show. That's why I couldn't wait for you."

"So who was it?" Samantha asked in an urgent whisper.

"I don't know!" Brittany said. "I sat for *hours* inside that greasy spoon, and the creep never even showed up!"

The bell rang, and the three girls started climbing the marble steps.

"Promise me you won't breathe a word of this to anyone," Brittany said as they entered the building.

"Any enemy of Nikki Masters is a friend of mine," Kim said, smiling.

"My lips are sealed," Samantha said.

"See you guys at lunch," Brittany called, heading down the hall to her locker. As she walked, she eyed everybody she passed. Any one of them could be the person who'd slipped her the note Friday night.

It was just one more thing to hate Nikki Masters for, Brittany mused as she reached her locker. Quickly she dialed the combination on her lock and flung open the door. She'd taped a small mirror to the inside of the door, and her reflection flew past her as the locker opened.

Pulling the metal door back toward herself, Brittany studied her reflection more closely. Lustrous dark hair framed her round face. Her dark eyes flashed, and her full mouth pouted prettily. Well, at least she was still gorgeous!

Brittany suddenly noticed a folded piece of paper sticking through a slit in the locker door. She grabbed the note and unfolded it.

Sorry I couldn't make it to Slim and Shorty's. Hope you enjoyed your cheeseburger and extra pickle, hold the onions! I'll be in touch.

Brittany's eyes widened in horror. How had the blackmailer known what she'd ordered Friday night? Had he or she been in the diner the whole time? Brittany tried to remember who'd been there, but no one came to mind. Everyone who counted had gone to the Loft after the show.

Brittany imagined a pair of evil, laughing eyes, furtively watching her every move. Then she shuddered. This blackmailer might be a real psycho!

2

Lacey Dupree felt like a criminal as she searched the halls at lunchtime for Tom. She hadn't seen him all morning. Even if she had seen him, she wasn't sure what she could have done about it. He'd finally agreed not to be seen in public with her until she'd told Rick about the two of them.

Lacey poked her head inside the cafeteria and took a quick look around. All she saw were long Formica tables filled with chattering students under buzzing fluorescent lights. Hugging the cinder-block wall, Lacey walked quickly past the first rows of tables, scanning the room for a black leather jacket, a lean, handsome face, and shaggy dark hair. No Tom.

A few tables back Lacey did see Nikki and Robin with their boyfriends, Tim Cooper and Calvin Roth. Calvin was one of Rick's best friends, which meant Rick couldn't be far away. Sure enough, Lacey spotted Rick coming out of the kitchen with a tray just then. She couldn't risk running into Tom with Rick around, so Lacey raced out the back door of the lunchroom.

The hallway was deserted. Tom's locker was just upstairs. Maybe he was there. Lacey pushed open the doors to the stairwell, but before she'd climbed the first step, she felt a hand grip her arm and pull her into the darkness beneath the stairs.

"Wha—?" Lacey started to say, but soft, feathery kisses covered her mouth, and strong arms reached around her waist, pulling her close.

Even with her eyes closed Lacey knew who it was. She could tell by the smooth leather jacket and thick hair, which brushed against her face. Lacey melted against Tom, lost in his kisses.

When they drew apart, Lacey studied Tom's face in the shadows. He had high cheekbones and deep-set, forest green eyes that were hard to read, unlike his brother Rick's open hazel ones. In his right ear he wore a single gold stud.

"Hi," Lacey said softly.

"Hi." Tom grinned, burying his fingers in Lacey's thick, wavy red hair.

"Did anyone see you?" Lacey asked.

Tom shook his head. "Nope."

"I'm sorry we have to sneak around like this," Lacey said with a sigh. "I hate hiding from everyone."

"Then why are we doing it?" Tom asked with a shrug. "Are you ashamed to be seen with me?"

Lacey shook her head vehemently. "Of course not!" she insisted. "You know that. I just can't face Rick yet. How do you think he'll feel, finding out I'm crazy about his brother?"

"How do you think *I* feel?" Tom asked.

Lacey wrapped her arms around Tom and squeezed him tightly. "I'm sorry," she said softly. "I'll tell him, I promise."

Tom gazed at her steadily. "If you don't tell Rick soon, I'll have to."

"Was that who I think it was?" Kim Bishop asked as she stirred the strawberries in her yogurt with a plastic spoon.

Samantha Daley, sitting next to Kim, was also staring at the back door of the cafeteria.

Brittany's dark eyes gleamed above the can of diet soda she was drinking. "The question isn't *who* that was, but why is she dressed that way? Something strange has happened to Miss Prissy Lacey Dupree."

"Rick was sitting all by himself at the talent show on Friday," Samantha said eagerly. "Maybe they had a fight."

Brittany shook her head. "There's more to it than that. She's acting like a completely different person."

"Oh, who cares about Lacey Dupree?" Kim said irritably as Jeremy Pratt approached their table. "I've got bigger problems."

"Is he still ignoring you?" Samantha asked sympathetically.

Kim sniffed and stuck her pointy nose in the air. *"I'm* ignoring *him,"* she said. "If he can't learn how to be supportive, then I don't need him as a boyfriend."

Jeremy casually paused at the end of their table and retied the sleeves of the crewneck sweater slung over his shoulders. Then, without so much as a hello, he continued on his way. Brittany noticed how busy Kim had become searching the bottom of her yogurt for more strawberries.

"Don't let him get you down," Brittany counseled Kim. She stood up from the table and stretched. "I've got to do some work on my article about the talent show. DeeDee wants to see it after school." Brittany wrote the most popular column in the school paper, "Off the Record." Her columns included hot student gossip, fashion, entertainment, music—everything that mattered.

"Too bad you can't write the *real* story of what happened backstage," Samantha said.

Brittany gave her friend a warning look. "Remember, that story is strictly confidential. Are you going to the Loft this afternoon?"

"Of course," Samantha replied with a shrug.

"Okay, see you there," Brittany said, picking up her books. She left the cafeteria and headed for the *Record* office. Again she found herself studying the faces of everyone she passed, seeking out her blackmailer. Several times she was sure she felt a pair of eyes watching her, but no one stepped forward.

As she reached the last hallway, someone tapped her on the shoulder. Turning, Brittany was startled to see Martin Ives, a skinny, geeky junior. Martin had bad skin and was a couple of inches shorter than Brittany.

Martin was president of the art club and a talented painter but didn't seem to know where to stop with his work. Lately he'd been painting everything: his clothes, his notebooks, even his hair. Right then his hair was dyed various shades of blue and green. It stuck up in tufts all over his head.

"Yes?" Brittany asked irritably. The last thing she wanted to do was waste time with a guy whose hair was the same color as the ocean.

"So, did you enjoy lunch today?"

"What are you talking about?" Brittany asked. This guy was definitely pathetic.

"They served spaghetti and meatballs," Martin said, grinning slyly. "It must be one of your favorite meals. You even eat it cold, out of your purse!" Martin's eyes danced with glee.

Brittany suddenly found it difficult to breathe. Her heart started pounding in fear and revulsion. She felt light-headed, as if she was about to faint.

Martin Ives was her blackmailer! Martin Ives, social nonentity, borderline midget, now had the power to humiliate her in front of the entire school! Brittany's whole world was collapsing.

Steadying herself against the wall, Brittany blinked rapidly and tried to think. There had to be a way out of this. There had to be something she could do to knock Martin off guard.

Then the Tate brain clicked into gear, and Brittany had the answer. Martin had had a wicked crush on her during their sophomore year. He'd shadowed her around school, afraid to speak to her. She hadn't spoken to him, either, of course.

But now was the perfect time to start. All she had to do was turn on the charm, and Martin would melt. She'd have him wrapped around her finger in no time.

"You know, Martin," Brittany said sweetly, gazing down into his eyes, "I'm very flattered that you've been sending me notes. And your jokes about the spaghetti are *so* humorous." She laughed a tinkly little laugh.

"It's no joke, Brittany," Martin said, ignoring her flirtatious tone. "I saw your dirty trick at the talent contest."

Brittany giggled and said, "Oh, that silly thing? It wasn't a trick at all. Nikki and I had worked that out in advance."

Martin sneered at Brittany. "You don't fool me, Brittany," he said. "Not your lie about the spaghetti and not your flirting with me, either."

"What do you want?" Brittany asked. "Money? You're wasting your time if you do, because I don't have any." Brittany had spent every cent she had getting into the country club. On the other hand, if money could buy her way out of this situation, maybe it would be worth working extra hours at her mother's flower shop, Blooms.

"I don't want money," Martin said. "I'm

much more creative than that. Ever since junior high I've watched you scheme and push people around. Now I'm going to show you what it feels like."

Brittany wanted to laugh. She wasn't scared anymore. If Martin Ives wanted to match wits with her, he was welcome to try, but he would fail. Nobody could outscheme Brittany Tate.

"Good luck," Brittany said, starting off.

"Not so fast," Martin warned, grabbing her arm again. "You haven't heard my plan."

Brittany rolled her eyes. "What?" she asked impatiently.

"You're going to go out with me, this afternoon," Martin said. "To the Loft."

Brittany laughed. "Why would I do that?"

"Because if you don't," Martin said, "I'll tell the entire school that you tried to sabotage Nikki and Tim's scene. Then everyone will see you for what you really are. And I'll go right to DeeDee Smith and tell her you were only pretending to write an article on the show so you could be backstage. I don't think she'd be too happy about that, do you?"

So, Martin was serious, and Brittany was stuck. But there was no way she'd show up at the Loft with him. What would Chip think? Chip Worthington, Brittany's superrich, supersnob on-again, off-again boyfriend, who went to Talbot, a private school in town. Brittany had one last hope to get Martin off her case.

"You know, Martin," Brittany said, "I wouldn't mind going out with you, but I don't think my super-jealous boyfriend would be very understanding. By the way, did I mention he's six feet tall, one hundred seventy pounds, and on the Talbot School football team? I'm afraid he won't be happy about any competition."

Martin shrugged. "I'll take my chances."

"Such courage," Brittany said icily, her mind working furiously. There had to be some way out of this. But just at that moment who should be heading straight for them but Nikki Masters!

"Well?" Martin asked, lifting an eyebrow in Nikki's direction. "Is it a date? Or do I start spreading the news?"

Brittany clenched her fists. She was stuck, at least for the moment. "Well, if you insist on living a lie, I'll go to the Loft with you."

"And you have to act as if you like me," Martin added. "That's part of the deal."

Brittany felt nauseated, but she couldn't refuse. "Certainly, *darling,*" she said, forcing the words through her gritted teeth. Martin Ives was going to be one very sorry guy.

3 ~~~

"You call this a column?" DeeDee snapped as she flipped through the typewritten pages Brittany had just handed her.

The *Record* office was small and cluttered. Several desks had been pushed together along one wall of the room. On one was a new computer; on the others were two old electric typewriters. A pasteup board filled another wall, and filing cabinets stuffed with fifty years' worth of back *Record* issues lined the third wall. The conference table took up the center of the room.

"Okay, so it's a rough draft," Brittany said. "I still have two more days until my deadline."

"You'll need two more *weeks* to revise

this," DeeDee said. "The whole thing's sloppy. And what happened to all the quotes you were supposed to get? I thought that was the whole point of going backstage."

DeeDee saw the smile plastered on Brittany's face, but she knew how upset Brittany really was. Brittany was an excellent writer, and her column wasn't even that bad, but for some reason DeeDee couldn't help but criticize her.

"I want this completely rewritten by tomorrow," DeeDee said, handing the pages back to Brittany. "Go find the people you talked to backstage, and get more quotes."

Brittany nodded silently and left the office. DeeDee checked the clock on the wall over the door. It was two-thirty. There was still work to be done, but DeeDee couldn't wait another minute to get home to see if the letter from Kingston had arrived.

Kingston was a very prestigious university, one of the oldest in the Northeast. DeeDee's grandfather had been one of the first black men ever to graduate from Kingston, so DeeDee felt doubly obligated to attend.

After grabbing her coat, DeeDee pushed through the office door, raced down the hall, and ducked out a side entrance. Her legs felt like jelly as she ran home. DeeDee marched up the stone walk to the two-story house and stopped on the porch in front of the black metal mailbox.

She lifted the lid of the mailbox and reached inside. The box was stuffed with rolled-up magazines and envelopes. DeeDee removed the huge stack of mail.

DeeDee didn't take the time to go inside. If the answer had arrived, she wanted to find out now. She sat down on the wooden bench beneath the mailbox and quickly pulled out all the magazines and glossy brochures.

DeeDee was so nervous that she didn't recognize the Kingston logo on the upper left-hand corner of the long white envelope at first. Going through the mail a second time, she gasped. This was it!

DeeDee felt the envelope. It seemed thin —too thin. If it were an acceptance, it would be fat because it would be filled with questionnaires and dorm applications and other information.

DeeDee ripped open the envelope and pulled out the single, folded sheet of paper. The same logo, a crest with two tigers facing each other, headed the page. The letter was just a few short paragraphs.

Taking a deep breath, DeeDee forced herself to read it. She hadn't been rejected. That was the good news. The bad news was that she hadn't been accepted, either. She'd been deferred. That meant she had to wait until the spring to find out if she'd get in.

It obviously didn't matter that she had top grades and was editor in chief of her school paper. Every other applicant to Kingston must have had credentials like those. There probably hadn't been anything special about her application at all, DeeDee decided.

She slumped against the back of the bench. As bad as she felt about not getting accepted, DeeDee knew this was going to hurt her father even more. He'd be shattered!

Stuffing the letter into her overcrowded purse, DeeDee gathered up the rest of the mail and her bookbag and let herself into the house. She dumped the mail on the hall table and wandered into the kitchen, still in her coat.

Realization started to grow inside her. It was really her father's dream for her to attend Kingston. Not hers.

Actually, there were a few colleges she liked better than Kingston. And it wasn't a coincidence that they all had programs in broadcast journalism, either. That was what DeeDee had always wanted to study, though she'd barely admitted it, even to herself. She knew her father wanted her to be a print journalist, like he was, but television news seemed so much more vital and exciting. Kingston offered excellent academics, but they didn't have any TV facilities.

DeeDee began to feel a glimmer of hope. Instead of feeling depressed, she was going to turn this situation to her advantage—and she knew exactly where she was going to start.

"So where'd you get the bucks for the jacket?" Robin Fisher asked Lacey. "I thought you were broke since you bought your car."

Lacey picked up her menu and pretended to read it. "Tom gave it to me," she mumbled.

The two girls were sitting in a booth at the Loft, waiting for Nikki. Formerly an artist's studio, the vast, high-ceilinged space was now a popular hangout for River Heights teens.

"Gee, the two of you really *are* close," Robin said. "You're even sharing clothes. Things are moving pretty fast, aren't they?"

"I'm happy with the way things are going," Lacey replied evenly.

"I don't get it," Robin said, shaking her head, her neon green lightning bolt earrings quivering.

But before Lacey could reply, Nikki Masters ran up to the table, breathless. "Sorry

I'm late. I hope you guys ordered without me."

"We're fine," Robin said with a shrug as Nikki sat down next to her.

Fine? Lacey thought, tears welling in her eyes. Ever since kindergarten she and Robin and Nikki had been best friends. They'd shared everything—toys, clothes, their deepest secrets. But now they were barely speaking.

Lacey decided it must be her fault. *She'd* been the one to avoid her friends. That meant it was up to her to mend things. But it was difficult to talk to them about Tom, especially since Robin had such a chip on her shoulder.

"Have you seen Tim?" Nikki asked. "He said he'd meet us here."

"Not yet," Lacey said. "I hope I see him before I have to leave for work."

"So what's new?" Nikki asked brightly, trying to ignore the obvious tension at the table.

"Oh, nothing much," Robin said, "except that Lacey's joined a biker gang."

"That's not fair, Robin!" Lacey cried.

"Come on," Nikki said, placing a hand on Robin's arm. "Lacey's been going through a tough time, and you're not making it any easier."

"*Lacey's* going through a tough time?"

Robin exclaimed. *"I'm* more upset about it than she is."

"I'm sorry you're so upset," Lacey began. "It feels like I've spent the entire day apologizing, but you have to understand——"

"How could you possibly choose Tom over Rick?" Robin interrupted. "Rick's such a great guy. And Tom's a low-life loser. I heard he's planning to drop out of school to be an auto mechanic."

"That's not true," Lacey shot back. "He *does* work in a garage after school, but he's not going to drop out. He just works to support his artistic career."

"Tom Stratton is an artist?" Nikki asked.

"He's not a painter, or anything like that," Lacey said. "Tom wants to be a musician. He's already playing in a band."

"To be an artist, you have to be sensitive. From what I hear, Tom Stratton is hardly sensitive. I heard he has a tattoo on his right shoulder."

"It's a really small one," Lacey said quickly.

Nikki's eyebrows shot up, and Robin gave a knowing smirk.

"Gee," Robin said, "things are moving even faster than we thought."

Lacey felt her face grow hot. "Anyway, the tattoo doesn't mean anything. Tom's just a nonconformist. You should understand that,

Robin. You don't like to look like anybody else, either."

"It's not just Tom's looks," Robin argued. "It's the way he acts. I mean, Tom Stratton barely says a word to anyone. Is he too macho to talk? And I heard that all his old girlfriends have been empty-headed bimbos."

"Robin—" Nikki warned.

"I don't mean *you,*" Robin said to Lacey. "I'm just warning you to watch out, that's all."

"You don't even know him!" Lacey cried, fighting back tears. "Everything you've heard is just rumor. Tom's a sweet, intelligent person, and he treats me wonderfully. Certainly better than Rick did. I'm not the one who broke up with Rick, remember? He started going out with Katie Fox."

"Then why all the secrecy if you're not dating Rick anymore?" Robin asked.

"It does seem a little strange," Nikki agreed. "There has to be some reason you're hiding this relationship from everyone. Are you afraid of something?"

Lacey sighed and took a tiny sip of her shake. "Maybe I *am* afraid of what people will think," she admitted. "I mean, Tom's not exactly president of the senior class. But that's not the reason we've been keeping things quiet. It's because we haven't told

Rick yet. And I don't want Rick to find out until I've had a chance to tell him myself."

"I think Rick has a right to know," Robin said, "especially since his ex-girlfriend is dating his brother."

"But I can see how it would be really hard to say something," Nikki said, turning to Lacey. "When Rick finds out, he might be furious, even if you two aren't going out anymore."

"I know, I know," Lacey said, nervously running her hands through her hair. "That's why I'd like you guys to keep this quiet until I speak to Rick myself."

Nikki sighed. "I won't tell. But I do think you should say something soon."

"Okay," Robin agreed. "I'll keep my mouth shut, too. But if this goes on much longer, I won't be able to face Rick without saying something. What you and Tom are doing just isn't fair—to anyone."

4

DeeDee pedaled furiously up the narrow, tree-lined road that led to the Westmoor University campus. The sun was setting, and the last tour of the day was starting in a few minutes. DeeDee didn't want to miss it. Westmoor was a local college with an excellent TV journalism program. DeeDee wanted to find out as much as possible about Westmoor. That way she'd have some ammunition when she gave her father the bad news about Kingston.

DeeDee reached a Georgian brick building with white shutters and a single white column on either side of the double front doors. A small group of people waited in front of the door. As DeeDee drew closer, she saw a sign next to the building that said Administration Parking Lot. According to the woman DeeDee had spoken with on the phone, this was where the tour would begin.

After locking up her bike, DeeDee walked toward the group. They were listening intently to a tall, good-looking student who spoke in a deep, resonant voice. Had the tour already started? DeeDee ran the last few yards.

"For the first few years this administration building was the only building on campus, and all classes were taught here. But as you'll see, Westmoor has expanded quite a bit since then. Please follow me." The tall young man grinned and gestured toward a nearby cluster of stone buildings.

DeeDee followed the group as they crossed the parking lot, her boots crunching in the gravel.

"These are some of the dormitories," the guide continued as the crowd reached the stone buildings. The buildings formed three sides of a square around a grassy lawn.

As DeeDee listened to the guide give a history of the dormitories, she began to realize that she wasn't listening so much to *what* he was saying as to *how*. His voice was so soothing and sexy. It occurred to DeeDee that she hadn't even gotten a good look at the guide's face since he was so much taller than everyone else.

DeeDee's eyes traveled up the tour guide's navy blue jacket, past his purple- and gold-striped scarf, and paused on his beautifully sculpted face. His skin was light brown, and he had high cheekbones, a strong chin, and warm brown eyes. His hair was razor-cut very short, and he smiled often as he spoke. No wonder the school had hired him to lead tours. He was a natural. DeeDee wondered what his name was and whether he had a girlfriend.

As DeeDee studied the young man, he turned his gaze to her and smiled even more warmly. DeeDee felt an electric current run through her body. Had he noticed her, too?

But why was she wondering about him in the first place? DeeDee was there on business, to gather information, not to flirt with some guy she'd never even met. DeeDee mentally shook herself for letting her mind wander.

"This is WWES, the campus television station," the guide said, leading them toward a brick building with a radar dish on the roof.

The guide led them into the lobby. "This is where communications students get hands-on experience—writing, producing, and ap-

pearing in their own television programs,"
the guide said. "TV journalism majors also
work in the studio, putting out two live news
broadcasts seven days a week."

DeeDee felt her heart beat faster as the
guide led them down a hall to a swinging
door marked Studio. The room was large,
with a jumble of lighting equipment, video
cameras, and cables snaking along the floor.

This was exactly the sort of journalism
program DeeDee wanted. Kingston, she
knew, had nothing like this. The idea of
staying in River Heights for a few more years
was beginning to sound more and more ap-
pealing.

An hour later DeeDee felt supercharged.
The television station had been state-of-the-
art, the academic buildings were charming,
the library was huge, and best of all, the tour
guide had smiled at her six times! He'd even
placed a gentle hand on her shoulder, just for
a second, as he led the crowd into the dining
commons.

DeeDee wasn't sure what to do. Should she
smile back and encourage him? Or was this
just part of his "charming guide" routine?
Maybe the university told him to be extra
nice to prospective students.

The guide led the crowd back to the parking lot. Then he thanked them for coming
and invited them to visit the Administration

Building for brochures and additional information. Most of the group headed to the building, but DeeDee lingered outside. The tour guide didn't seem to notice. He was busy talking to the mother of one of the girls in his polite, professional voice.

It must have been her imagination. What would a college guy see in a high school student? He'd probably led so many tours that he didn't even notice anyone individually. Embarrassed, DeeDee turned away and headed toward the double doors of the Administration Building.

"Excuse me." The voice was unmistakable. It was the same deep voice she'd been listening to for nearly an hour. DeeDee turned around slowly.

The handsome young guide was staring down at her with liquid brown eyes.

"Yes?" DeeDee asked nervously.

The guide stared at his feet, which DeeDee now noticed were rather large and encased in white, high-top basketball sneakers. Could he possibly be shy?

"Uh, I was wondering if you had any more questions about the school," he said.

DeeDee's heart missed a beat. Maybe this guy had noticed her after all! "Well, yes," she said, thinking fast. "I guess I missed the beginning of the tour, so I don't know what you said in the first couple of minutes."

"You missed the part where I introduced myself," the young man said, grinning. He extended his hand. "I'm Toby Jackson, and I'm a freshman here."

"DeeDee Smith," DeeDee said as her small hand was swallowed up in his larger one. "I'm a senior at River Heights High."

"So you live around here?" Toby asked.

DeeDee nodded toward her bike. "Fifteen minutes, on my own steam."

Toby smiled and pointed to the stone buildings around the quad that had been the first stop on the tour. "I live in the dorms over there. That means we're practically neighbors."

"Practically," DeeDee said, returning his smile. She could hardly believe this was happening.

"So tell me, neighbor," Toby said, "would you be interested in seeing more of Westmoor? We have a very good coffee shop, right here on campus. They make a mean cup of cappuccino."

DeeDee had never had a cappuccino in her life, but she wasn't going to let that stop her. "Well, I should be getting home pretty soon," she said coolly, "but I do have lots of questions about the school. Where did you say that coffee shop was?"

*   *   *

"You don't have to squeeze my arm so tight," Brittany complained, trying to shake Martin's bony fingers off the sleeve of her coat.

"I just want to make sure you're not going to run away," Martin said as the two of them walked across the parking lot of the Loft.

"A deal's a deal," Brittany said grimly. "You keep your mouth shut, and I'll pretend you don't turn my stomach."

Martin's dark eyes looked so wounded that Brittany almost felt sorry for him. Then she reminded herself what he was doing to her.

"I'm not so bad, once you get to know me," Martin said stiffly. "But I guess you never look past the surface, do you?"

"What's that supposed to mean?" Brittany asked, pausing by the entrance of the restaurant and pulling her compact out of her purse. Quickly she reapplied her blush. As long as she had to be seen with Martin Ives, she wanted to make sure that she looked good.

"Never mind," Martin said, pulling her inside. "Let's just hope all your friends— and enemies—are here so they can see us together."

As the battered wooden door slammed shut behind them, Brittany was sure that all eyes were turned on her. Kim and Samantha, sitting at a paint-splattered table with Kyle Kirkwood, waved at Brittany and gave her sympathetic looks. Brittany had confided in them. Jeremy Pratt, still ignoring Kim, sat a few tables away with two of his snobby friends, Hal Evans and Wayne Yates.

Worst of all, at the far end of the open space, Nikki Masters sat with Tim Cooper. Her two sidekicks, Spacey Lacey and Robin the Moose, were just leaving.

The last people Brittany wanted to see right then were Nikki and Tim, but no way was Martin going to miss out on this opportunity.

He was rubbing his hands together with glee. "Where shall we start?"

"You know, Martin," Brittany said, "I've got this terrible headache. Maybe we could come back here tomorrow, when I'm feeling better."

"Let's go visit your girlfriends," Martin said, ignoring her. "Kyle's a buddy of mine, anyway."

Brittany remembered that Samantha's boyfriend had been pretty nerdy before Samantha made him over with a new haircut and some decent clothes.

"Martin!" Kyle called, waving them over. "What are you doing here? Is the Loft having another show of your paintings?"

Brittany looked at Martin and frowned.

The Loft sometimes sold artwork by local artists, but Martin was pretty young to be exhibiting his paintings already.

Martin shook his head modestly as he stopped by Kim, Samantha, and Kyle's table. "My next show's not until next month," he said, "and it's going to be at the Madison Gallery, downtown."

"Cool," Kyle said. "I hope you'll send me an invite."

"Definitely," Martin said.

"So why don't you guys sit down?" Kyle said. "I'm sure you girls have a lot to catch up on. You haven't seen each other in hours."

"Ordinarily, we'd take you up on that," Martin said, taking Brittany's hand. "But we have to move on. I told Nikki and Tim we'd hang out with them this afternoon."

Brittany shot Kim and Samantha a pleading look, but there was nothing they could do to save her. Dragging her feet, Brittany allowed Martin to lead her across the restaurant. Nikki and Tim sat next to each other, all lovey-dovey, talking to Ellen Ming and Karen Jacobs, who were standing by their booth.

"I *loved* your performance," Ellen was saying. A slender girl with black hair and bangs, Ellen was the junior class treasurer. "It was the best part of the show!"

"I laughed so much," Karen added enthusiastically. "You two were hysterical!" Karen was a junior who dated Ben Newhouse, the junior class president. She was the layout and production editor for the *Record*. She was also Brittany's main competition for the editor in chief position on the paper after DeeDee graduated.

Nikki beamed at all the compliments, and Tim squeezed her tighter.

Brittany shuddered inside. She had actually contributed to their success! Just thinking about it was like pouring vinegar into a paper cut, and her leather bag would never be the same.

"Nikki! Tim!" Martin greeted them. "Brittany and I just wanted to add our congratulations to everyone else's."

Brittany noticed Nikki and Tim exchange a surprised look. Karen and Ellen also eyed Brittany and Martin curiously. Brittany wanted to sink through the floor, embarrassed.

"I'm glad you liked the scene," Nikki said sweetly.

"You know," Martin said, running his fingers through his green and blue hair, "I had a question about it, actually."

Brittany stiffened.

"See, I've read *The Blue Moon Luncheonette,*" he said. "If I remember correctly, Rita is supposed to throw a plate of spaghetti at Lamont. I was wondering how you came up with the idea to throw a bucket of water instead."

"Well, actually," Nikki said, "we didn't plan it in advance."

"What Nikki means," Tim said, "was that someone *swiped* our plate of spaghetti, and Nikki had to improvise with water. It made the scene."

"You're kidding!" Martin said, pretending to act shocked. "You mean somebody actually stole one of your props?"

Brittany felt Martin's fingers squeeze hers. Her own hand was trembling, but she tried not to appear nervous.

"It *was* a dirty trick," Tim agreed.

"It was worse than that, if you ask me," Martin said. "It was *sick.* What kind of warped individual would do such a thing? And how could anyone have hidden an entire plate of spaghetti? That must have gotten pretty messy."

Brittany was dying to stick her fingernails into the back of Martin's hand, but she didn't dare. Everyone might guess that Martin was talking about her. Instead, all she could do was smile like an idiot and wish the Loft offered an Arsenic Rat-Poison Shake so she could serve it to Martin.

5 ⌇

As DeeDee entered the Westmoor Café, she was enveloped by warm air and the smell of fresh coffee and bittersweet chocolate. Classical music was playing under the murmur of voices and the clatter of dishes.

"Not bad, huh?" Toby said, following DeeDee into the café. "It's hard to believe this place is run by the same people who run the dining commons. The food here is actually good!"

DeeDee laughed. "I've heard about dining hall food. Is it as bad as they say?"

"It's not *that* bad," Toby reassured her. "It's just not as good as my mother's cooking, but then, nothing is."

Toby led DeeDee to an empty table, helped

her take off her coat, then held her chair for her while she sat down. He certainly was a gentleman. There weren't many guys at River Heights High with such sophisticated manners.

A cheerful young waitress dropped some handwritten menus on their table. "I'll be right back to take your order," she said.

The menu listed ten different kinds of coffee, four types of hot chocolate, and a dozen tempting desserts. When the waitress returned, Toby ordered cappuccino and chocolate cake.

DeeDee wasn't sure what to order. Her stomach was doing disturbing little flip-flops, like an acrobat gone haywire. Why did she feel so nervous? Yes, Toby was a gorgeous college guy, but she was perfectly capable of handling herself.

"I'll have a hot chocolate," DeeDee told the waitress.

"So how do you like Westmoor so far?" Toby asked when the woman had left.

"I love it," DeeDee replied immediately. "I can't believe I've lived in town all my life and never took a tour of the campus."

"I'm glad you took *my* tour," Toby said.

Toby was definitely flirting with her, DeeDee knew, but maybe he was just a smooth operator. DeeDee decided to proceed with caution.

"So," Toby went on, "what other colleges have you applied to besides Westmoor?"

"Actually," DeeDee said, "the only application I've sent in so far is to Kingston University. But I found out today that I was deferred, so I really have to get cracking now and see where else I can still apply."

"Is Westmoor high on your list?" Toby asked.

"Very," DeeDee said. "You've got a great journalism program here, and that's what I'm most interested in. What are *you* majoring in?"

"I'm still a freshman, so I don't have to declare a major yet," Toby said, "but I'm planning to study business and go on to get my M.B.A.——if I don't get drafted by the NBA." He grinned.

"You're a basketball player?" DeeDee asked.

Toby nodded. "I'm a forward."

"That's great!" DeeDee said. "Not many freshmen get to play varsity."

The waitress appeared with a tray and unloaded two steaming mugs and a slice of chocolate cake inches thick.

"Want some?" Toby asked, offering her a bite of the cake. DeeDee shook her head. "So let's get back to you," Toby said. "Are you disappointed that you didn't get into Kingston?"

DeeDee sipped her hot chocolate thoughtfully. "It's funny," she said, putting down the mug. "I always thought I wanted to go to Kingston, but I'm beginning to think I'd be happier if I went somewhere else, like Westmoor."

Toby smiled broadly. "Then I'm going to do everything in my power to convince you to come here. I'll be your personal Westmoor ambassador. If there's anything you need to know or anything you want to see, just let me know."

"I'm honored," DeeDee said with a grin. Then she checked her watch. "It's almost six!" she exclaimed. "I'd better get moving."

Toby rose from his chair and put some money on the table. "Let me drive you home," he said.

"I have my bike," DeeDee told him.

"I have a bike rack," Toby said with a shrug. "Come on. It's dark out."

As Toby pulled up in front of the Smiths' house a few minutes later, DeeDee felt a sinking feeling in her stomach. Her father's car was in the driveway. That meant she'd have to face him as soon as she walked in the house.

Toby shifted into Park and turned off the ignition. "It really was nice meeting you."

DeeDee turned to Toby and smiled. "Thanks for the hot chocolate."

Toby cleared his throat. "Um, DeeDee," he said, "would you like to go out with me again tomorrow night? I know a great diner downtown. It's a fifties place, so it has a jukebox and a dance floor with Hula-Hoops and a real fifty-seven Thunderbird convertible parked right in the middle."

"I'd love to!" DeeDee said. "But it's a school night, so I'll have to ask my parents."

"I think I can live with that," Toby said. "How about if I pick you up around seven o'clock?"

"Perfect," DeeDee said.

Toby tore a piece of paper out of a spiral notebook in the back seat and scribbled something down. "Here's my number. If there's a problem, just call me. Otherwise, I'll see you tomorrow night."

DeeDee grinned. "I hope so." She and Toby got out of the car, and he unfastened her bike from the rack on the roof. Then, as if it were light as a feather, Toby lifted her bicycle down and placed it on the sidewalk.

"Thanks for everything," DeeDee said, holding on to the handlebars of her bike.

Toby smiled at her. "See you tomorrow." With a few long strides he was back beside the car.

As Toby pulled his car out of the driveway, DeeDee slowly walked her bicycle into the garage. She couldn't even enjoy the thrill of knowing a great guy was interested in her. She was too worried about what was going to happen when she faced her father.

"I'm home!" DeeDee called as she entered the kitchen from the garage.

"We're in the living room!" Mrs. Smith called back.

As DeeDee cut through the front hall, she saw the stack of mail scattered all over the table. Her parents must have searched for the letter from Kingston when they got home. They hadn't found it, of course. It was safely hidden in DeeDee's purse.

"Well?" Mr. Smith asked as DeeDee entered the living room. He sat in his easy chair, wearing an old Kingston sweatshirt. It was gray and faded and pulled across his large stomach. Mrs. Smith was standing behind her husband.

"Well, what?" DeeDee asked, trying to stall.

"I didn't see a letter from Kingston in the mail," Mr. Smith said. "I thought maybe you'd opened it and were waiting to give us the news in person."

DeeDee felt her heart lurch in her chest as she studied her father's face carefully. All she saw was a sweet, hopeful expression. He didn't know about the deferral. How could she disappoint him? She had to figure out a gentle way to break it to him, but she needed time.

Taking a deep breath, DeeDee crossed her fingers and said, "I wish I had something to tell you, but I haven't heard anything yet."

6

Tuesday morning Brittany stepped off the schoolbus, ready to dash for a side entrance of the school. She had decided, for the next few days, at least, to steer clear of Martin Ives. Hoisting her bookbag onto her shoulder, Brittany started to run, but a bony hand on her shoulder stopped her.

"Brittany!" said Martin loudly. "I thought you'd never get here!"

Brittany skidded to a halt. "Martin!" she replied halfheartedly. She turned and searched his beady eyes, trying to figure out what he wanted. Was he going to thank her for appearing at the Loft with him and tell her she was off the hook now?

"Let me carry your bookbag for you," Martin offered.

Brittany gritted her teeth. "It's not necessary. I'm perfectly capable of carrying it, thank you."

"But I *insist,*" Martin said, flashing an even row of pearly white teeth. Fangs, Brittany corrected herself.

"Look, Martin," Brittany said in a low voice as they walked toward the school, "didn't you humiliate me enough yesterday? Everyone in school saw us together. What more do you want to prove?"

"That yesterday wasn't a fluke. That we're a couple."

Brittany groaned. "No one will ever believe that, no matter how much you follow me."

"They'll believe it," Martin insisted. "They just need to see us together often enough." He placed his fingers against Brittany's back and guided her toward the steps where Kim and Samantha were standing.

Brittany hid a smile. Martin didn't realize that Kim and Samantha knew what was really going on. This could be fun.

"Hi, girls," Martin said confidently, ignoring their confused expressions. "Britty and I thought we'd say hello."

Britty? Now, *that* Brittany totally hated.

"Oh, yes," Brittany said brightly. "We

couldn't go inside without seeing you." She gave her friends a big wink.

Kim turned her pointy nose toward Martin. "You know," she said in her cool, aloof voice, "you two make the *cutest* couple."

"Oh, don't I know it, too," Samantha cooed in her best southern-belle accent. "I've been noticing Martin myself. Why, if I didn't have Kyle, I'd be after him like a bear chasing honey."

Brittany saw a blush rise to Martin's blemished face. He was buying it!

Martin seemed very pleased. "Well, I've got to get going." After giving Brittany a quick peck on the cheek, he headed up the steps.

Brittany dug into her bag for a tissue and scrubbed at her cheek. "Gross!" she said. "But you two were really great."

"I can't believe you're still letting him get away with this," Samantha said. "Isn't there anything you can do?"

"Really," Kim agreed. "He's so . . . unsightly. His complexion has more craters than the moon!"

"I'm working on it," Brittany assured them. "But let's change the subject, okay? Where's Jeremy?"

Kim tossed her blond hair back over her shoulder and heaved a short sigh. "I wouldn't know. I still haven't spoken to him."

Brittany turned to Samantha. "Things with Kyle seem to be going well?"

Samantha nodded. "I haven't seen much of him lately, though. He's working on some secret project."

"Oh?" Brittany asked with interest. She loved secrets. Especially if she could be the one to spill them in her column.

"He hasn't told me a thing about it," Samantha went on. "Except that everyone in school will know about it soon."

"Hmmm," Brittany said. She made a mental note to be friendlier to Kyle. Even though he was Samantha's boyfriend, he wasn't anybody really important.

Whatever he was working on, Brittany wanted to make sure she found out before Karen Jacobs did. Getting a scoop on a big article would be one more way she could impress Mr. Greene, the *Record*'s faculty adviser, before he decided who would replace DeeDee as editor in chief.

Brittany smiled to herself. Martin Ives might have brought her down for the moment, but Brittany Tate would rise again!

"I'm home!" Lacey called as she entered the kitchen through the back door. She threw her car keys on the counter.

Mrs. Dupree, wearing an apron over her business suit, was setting the table. Her red hair, a few shades lighter than Lacey's, was short and fluffy, and her pale blue eyes peered at Lacey from behind brown, horn-rimmed glasses. Her father, Lacey knew, would still be at work.

"Hi, dear," Mrs. Dupree said pleasantly but without her usual warmth. Since Lacey had come home last Friday on Tom's motorcycle, the two of them hadn't spoken much. Lacey's mom had forbidden her to see Tom again, but Lacey was still seeing him.

It was the first time Lacey had ever actually lied to her mother. She wasn't proud of herself, but she couldn't let go of Tom. She already cared too much about him. On the other hand, she couldn't spend the rest of her life hiding the truth from her mother.

"I'll make the salad," Lacey offered.

Mrs. Dupree smiled at Lacey for the first time in days. "That's very thoughtful of you."

For a few moments they worked in silence, Lacey washing lettuce, and Mrs. Dupree chopping onions.

"How's Rick?" Mrs. Dupree asked, sniffling from the onions.

Lacey handed her mother a tissue from the box on the windowsill above the sink. "I've been wanting to talk to you about Rick—and something else."

Lacey pulled the lettuce apart, into bite-size pieces, and threw them in the big wooden salad bowl. "Actually, Rick and I broke up, and he's already seeing someone else."

"Oh, honey!" Mrs. Dupree said, putting down her chopping knife and tissue to give Lacey a hug. "That's awful. I know you must be hurting right now."

Lacey let her head rest, briefly, on her mother's shoulder. "It was pretty hard," she said softly. "It still is, a little. But that's not all I wanted to talk to you about."

"Oh?" Mrs. Dupree straightened up and began chopping again. "Don't tell me it has something to do with that hoodlum on the motorcycle. I didn't like the look of him at all. You haven't been riding around with him after I specifically told you not to?"

"No," Lacey said honestly. "I haven't been on his motorcycle."

"Good," Mrs. Dupree said. "No matter how angry you are with Rick, there's no reason to do something self-destructive."

"What's self-destructive?" Lacey asked angrily, shredding the lettuce into tiny specks. "The guy or the motorcycle?"

"Well, both," said Mrs. Dupree. "And we don't even know who this Tom person is."

Lacey gave her mother a sideways glance

and tried not to smile. "It's not like he comes from a family like the Strattons."

Mrs. Dupree nodded. "That's right."

"A nice, acceptable family with responsible, loving parents and strong values."

"Exactly," Mrs. Dupree said. "You may laugh and think I'm old-fashioned, but those things are important to me."

Lacey faced her mother dead-on. "Well, have you ever really talked to Mrs. Stratton?" she demanded. "Because if you had, you'd know that she has two sons—Rick and *Tom.*"

Mrs. Dupree went on chopping for a moment, as if she hadn't heard. Then, gradually, the knife slowed in its regular, hacking movement and froze against the wooden cutting board. Mrs. Dupree stared at Lacey, trying to comprehend. "Wait a minute," she said. "Do you mean to tell me—"

Lacey nodded. "That that Tom person is Rick Stratton's brother!"

Mrs. Dupree's mouth fell open. She shut it again quickly. "Why didn't you tell me?" she asked. "Instead of leading me into a trap?"

"I wasn't trying to trap you," Lacey said, wiping her hands on a paper towel. "Well, maybe I was, but it was just to prove a point. Tom may drive a motorcycle and wear a leather jacket, but that's no reason to judge him by those things. He's a sweet, caring, considerate person."

Mrs. Dupree shook her head. "But he's Rick's brother," she said. "Are you doing this to get back at Rick?"

"No!" Lacey insisted. "It was a coincidence that I got to know Tom at all, honest. My car broke down and—" Lacey felt the tears she'd been suppressing for days suddenly burst from her eyes. "If only you could meet Tom and talk to him, you'd see why I like him so much." Lacey covered her face with her hands and sobbed.

Mrs. Dupree sighed. "Oh, Lacey," she said, placing a comforting arm around her daughter's shoulders. "I guess I haven't made this any easier on you, have I?"

Too upset to reply, Lacey only shook her head.

"Okay," Mrs. Dupree said. "If you want us to meet Tom, we'll meet him. Why don't you invite him over for dinner on Thursday night?"

Lacey looked at her mother in surprise. "Really?" she asked. "You'd do that for me?"

"You're our only child," Mrs. Dupree said. "We want you to be happy. And if this Tom person—if *Tom*—is as nice as you say he is, then I'm willing to admit I was wrong."

"Oh, Mom!" Lacey cried, throwing her arms around her mother. "You're the best."

Mrs. Dupree smoothed Lacey's hair. "But if I ever hear you've been on that motorcycle of his, you'll see my dark side, understand?"

Lacey nodded. "I'll call and invite Tom right now."

She bounded over to the phone mounted on the wall by the back door. As she punched out the familiar numbers on the phone, her heart suddenly constricted in fear. What if Rick answered?

But it was Tom's low, sexy voice that said hello. A few minutes later she was whistling as she chopped carrots for the salad. Tom had accepted the dinner invitation and asked her to go out tomorrow night to South of the Border. Maybe there was hope for the two of them after all!

7 ⌒⌒

When the Smiths' doorbell rang at five to seven on Tuesday, DeeDee was up in her room applying the finishing touches to her makeup. Toby was early, but DeeDee was prepared. She'd laid out her clothes, shoes, and even her makeup before school that day.

"DeeDee!" her mother called from downstairs. "Your date is here!"

DeeDee gave herself one last look in her full-length mirror. Since Toby was taking her to a fifties diner, she'd dressed appropriately in slim, salmon pink slacks, a black sweater, and a wide black belt. DeeDee was glad the outfit flattered her slender figure.

"DeeDee!" her mother called again.

"Coming!" After stepping into black

patent-leather flats, DeeDee dashed out of her room and down the stairs.

Mr. Smith was standing in the front hall, his arms crossed as he glared up at Toby. Toby was standing inside the front door, a small bunch of flowers in his hand. Had something gone wrong? Why was her father staring at Toby like that?

"Hi!" DeeDee smiled at Toby as she came down the last few steps.

Toby's worried expression disappeared. "Hi!" he said, holding out the flowers.

"Thanks!" DeeDee said.

"Do you want me to put those in water for you?" Mrs. Smith offered from the entrance to the kitchen. "I'm sure you two want to get going."

"Now, wait just a minute," Mr. Smith said. "Not so fast. I was just getting to know Toby here. DeeDee, why didn't you mention that your young man is a *jock?*"

The way he said the word, he might as well have said *jerk.* Mr. Smith couldn't have cared less about sports. He thought all athletes were morons. The only things he considered important were politics, world affairs, language, and her getting into Kingston University.

"He's also a business major," DeeDee said.

Mr. Smith shrugged. "So either way, college is a means to an end. Well, I guess that's the way it is these days," he said, backing off a bit. "Young people today are more concerned with their future careers than what they can learn from books."

"Not everyone is a bookworm like you," Mrs. Smith reminded her husband, slipping an arm around his waist. "When my husband and I started dating," she told Toby, "he only took me to the library."

DeeDee smiled at her mom and grabbed Toby's arm, practically pushing him out the door.

"Have her home by ten-thirty," Mr. Smith called after them as they headed down the front walk.

"Sorry about that," DeeDee said when they reached the car. "I don't know why my dad was being so rude. He's probably just grumpy because he thinks we haven't heard from Kingston yet."

"You mean you haven't told him?" Toby asked after he got in and started the car.

DeeDee sighed. "I've been trying to figure out just the right way to break the news to him. I thought it would be easier on him — and me — that way. But the longer I wait, the more tense we both get. I'm afraid you bore the brunt of that tonight."

"I've got strong shoulders," Toby said in his deep, resonant voice. "If there's anything I can do to help, just tell me."

DeeDee felt so comfortable with Toby, as if nothing bad could happen to her with him. She wondered what it would be like to feel his arms around her.

As if he'd read her thoughts, Toby reached one long arm across the back of the front seat and let it rest lightly, tentatively, on DeeDee's shoulder as he drove. DeeDee could tell he wasn't completely sure of himself. Knowing this made her feel even more relaxed.

Outside in the parking lot DeeDee shivered a little, and Toby wrapped his arm around her, pulling her against him.

"Is that better?" he asked.

DeeDee gazed up at him and nodded. "Much," she said.

The pink and blue neon sign over the door said Checkers. Inside, overstuffed leather booths lined the walls, and waitresses in circle skirts and saddle shoes carried stainless steel trays piled high with burgers and french fries.

Parked in the center of the floor was a bright red convertible. A DJ sat behind the wheel, working the stereo system that had been installed in place of the dashboard.

Around the car young couples were dancing and trying to keep spinning Hula-Hoops aloft.

"This is great!" DeeDee exclaimed as the hostess seated them at a booth in the back.

Toby gazed at her warmly. DeeDee wondered how it was possible that just being with someone could make her so happy.

After they'd ordered, Toby took DeeDee's hand in his. His touch sent a shiver up her arm. "You know," he said, "when you joined my tour yesterday, I got really flustered because you're so pretty. I almost forgot my speech, and I've given it about fifty times!"

DeeDee gave Toby a skeptical smile. "Do you always sweet-talk girls like this?" she asked.

Toby looked startled. "That wasn't sweet talk. That was a confession. I've meant everything I've said, believe me."

DeeDee quickly changed the subject. "So tell me more about your family. Where are you from?"

"Philadelphia," Toby said. "I grew up on the outskirts of the city."

"And what do your parents do?"

"My dad owns a taxi company. It's not very big, only about fifteen cars, but he does pretty well for himself. My mom doesn't work, but she's really involved with our church, and like I said, she's a great cook."

"Do you have any brothers or sisters?"

"Hey, wait a minute," Toby said. "I know you're a journalist, but this is sounding more like an interview than a conversation. If I answer this question, do you promise you'll tell me more about you?"

DeeDee laughed. "It's a deal."

The food came, and time flew as their conversation jumped from one topic to another. They discovered that they were both crazy about Chinese food, science fiction movies, and the novels of Thomas Hardy.

By the time ten o'clock rolled around, DeeDee felt as if they hadn't even scratched the surface. There was so much more she wanted to say to Toby, so many questions she wanted to ask, but she had to be home by ten-thirty.

The more she thought about it, the more DeeDee couldn't wait to go to college. Then she could stay out as late as she wanted. And if she went to Westmoor, she could see Toby any night without worrying that her father would scare him away. Of course, that was no reason to choose a university. DeeDee knew she had to make her decision on academic programs, not him. Still, Westmoor was looking better all the time.

"This evening went too fast," Toby said as he pulled up in front of the Smith house. It was five minutes to eleven.

DeeDee nodded. "I feel like we just left, and I'm back home already!"

"Well, then," Toby said, "we'll have to do this again sometime. How about Thursday?" he added. "I've got a game tomorrow night. Or you could come to the game, and we could go out afterward."

"There's no way I could go out two nights in a row," DeeDee said, "but Thursday might be okay."

"Hey," Toby said, "did you know the Westmoor basketball team is playing the River Heights High varsity squad on Saturday afternoon? It's an exhibition game for River Heights United Charities."

DeeDee nodded. "I have to assign a reporter to cover it."

"Does that mean *you* won't be going?" Toby asked, sounding disappointed.

"I never said that," DeeDee replied with a grin. Was Toby really asking her out for two more dates this week?

"Then you *are* going," Toby said definitively. "Come watch us play, and we can spend the rest of the day together."

"That sounds nice," DeeDee said softly, studying Toby from under her lashes. His face was half in shadow and half illuminated by the streetlight above the car.

"Just nice?" Toby asked, sliding a little closer to her.

"More than nice," DeeDee answered. Her heart was beating rapidly, and she felt her blood fizz as his face bent toward hers. DeeDee closed her eyes and felt the softest, sweetest sensation as his lips brushed over hers. Then Toby gathered her in his arms and pressed her against him.

DeeDee's head was spinning. Things were moving fast with Toby, but she didn't have the slightest desire to slow them down.

8 ⌇⌇

"Brittany!" a voice called from down the hall the next afternoon. It was the same voice that had been plaguing Brittany for the past two days.

Brittany raced desperately for the *Record* office, hoping to reach it before Martin caught up with her. DeeDee had called a newspaper staff meeting, and usually Brittany found the meetings a bore, but that day she couldn't wait to get away from Martin.

"Brittany!"

The voice was getting closer. Nearly colliding with several kids, Brittany raced around a corner and down the hall that led to the *Record* office. Just a few more yards and she'd be home free. And early. DeeDee was always complaining that the staff was late for meetings. Maybe Brittany could earn some brownie points.

Brittany was at the door of the office with her hand on the doorknob. Before she could turn it, though, Martin Ives reached in front of her and put his hand on hers. She was trapped!

"Going somewhere?" Martin asked.

Brittany wanted to scream, but she composed her face into a tranquil expression before she turned around. "Why, hello, Martin. You *know* I'd love to be with you, but unfortunately, I have a meeting."

"This will just take a minute," Martin said. "I wanted to ask you something."

Brittany tried to appear patient. "Yes?"

"Did you hear about the basketball game at Westmoor this Saturday?"

"Of course I've heard about it," Brittany snapped. *"Everybody's* going."

"Exactly," Martin said. "Including you and me."

"Oh, no," Brittany said, backing away a step. "You can't make me go to the game with you. There'll be so many people there. Besides, I already have a date with Chip Worthington, who is still my *real* boyfriend, just in case you're starting to believe this fantasy we're living."

"Of course I don't believe it," Martin said irritably. "You still don't get it, do you?"

"Why don't you explain it to me," Brittany said, "since I'm beginning to lose patience with you and this stupid game."

"You haven't suffered enough," Martin said simply. "Until you do, we're going to be stuck together like glue."

"Ugh," Brittany said before she could stop herself. She ignored Martin's glare. "You don't *know* how much I've suffered."

"Believe me, Brittany, I do," Martin answered. His expression was sad, but Brittany was too angry to feel sorry for him. A hardness crept back into his eyes then. "I'm still in charge," he said. "And I say you're going to break your date with Chip and go to the game with me. Or else."

"Or else what?" Brittany demanded defiantly.

"Or else maybe I'll pay Sasha Lopez a visit. You know those caricatures she draws for the paper? How'd you like to see one of you, backstage, with all those gooey spaghetti strands dripping out of your purse?"

Brittany pressed her lips together. "DeeDee would never run a picture like that. That would be using the newspaper to humiliate a student, and she would be too ethical to do something like that."

"She still might be interested in hearing about your little escapade," Martin said, "especially since you were supposed to be working on an article at the time."

Just then, Brittany spotted DeeDee marching down the hall toward them. "Shh!" she told Martin. "DeeDee might hear you."

"Then make it sound convincing," Martin said. Loudly he asked, "So, are we going to the Westmoor game on Saturday?"

Brittany tried to smile, though it felt more like gritting her teeth. "Of course."

DeeDee brushed past them, seeming not even to notice they were there. After DeeDee had disappeared inside the *Record* office, Martin gave a quick wave. "I'll be waiting for you at the bus tomorrow morning, bright and early."

"I can't wait," Brittany said sourly. Then she leaned against the wall in disgust and despair. This had gone on long enough. She *couldn't* break another date with Chip. Chip was already acting as if he suspected she was up to something.

On the other hand, Brittany couldn't break her date with Martin, or he'd sabotage her chances of becoming editor in chief next year. Brittany wanted to scream. There had to be a way out of this mess, but she couldn't go to the same game with two guys.

Or could she? Brittany smiled as a beautiful plan sprang fully formed into her brain. That was the answer. She'd go with *both* of them. Of course, each would have to think she was going with him alone. She could have Martin pick her up at home and tell Chip she'd meet him at the game. And she'd have to make sure they sat on opposite ends of the stadium. True, she'd have to do a lot of running back and forth, but it might just work.

"You want to fight dirty?" Brittany muttered to Martin's retreating back. "Okay, you're on."

DeeDee dumped her books on the conference table in the middle of the room. Karen Jacobs was sitting at the pasteup board, arranging photographs on a mock-up of next week's cover page. Her hair was pulled back in a loose French braid, and she wore a bright green sweater that played up her hazel eyes. Karen had been paying particular attention to her appearance these days, but DeeDee was too tired to give Karen a compliment.

"Where *is* everybody?" DeeDee asked irritably. "The meeting's supposed to start in two minutes, Brittany's out in the hall flirting, and who knows where everyone else is? Doesn't anybody care about this paper except me? And you, of course, Karen."

"They'll be here," Karen said calmly.

DeeDee knew she was overreacting, but she didn't care. She had a pounding headache. It was Wednesday, and she still hadn't told her father the bad news.

He had threatened to call Kingston that morning to find out why they were taking so long with their decision. That meant time was running out. DeeDee had to tell her father herself before he found out some other way. No wonder her head was pounding.

Kevin Hoffman, his red hair wild and unruly, strutted into the *Record* office, a huge grin on his freckled face. "I just got a great idea for my humor column," he said, pointing his thumb toward the hallway. "Brittany Tate and Martin Ives. Did you ever hear anything so funny in your entire life? I think I'm going to call it 'Believe it or Not.'"

"Very funny," DeeDee snapped. "Why don't you pour a little more creative energy into your column? Your last few articles haven't exactly been a barrel of laughs."

Frowning, Kevin took a seat at the table as Sasha Lopez breezed in. As usual, she was dressed all in black and was carrying a sketchbook under her arm.

"I've got a great caricature for this week's issue," Sasha said, opening up the sketchbook and showing it to DeeDee. The picture, a spoof of Nikki and Tim's scene from the

Talent Show, depicted Tim dripping wet, while Nikki looked on, holding an empty bucket.

DeeDee snorted with laughter. "Now *that's* funny," she said. Then she turned angrily to Brittany Tate and the other late-comers who had straggled in behind Sasha. "Very nice of you guys to show up," she remarked. "I hope your responsibilities to the *Record* haven't interfered in any way with your valuable social lives. Has anyone besides Sasha finished his or her assignment, or are you all late as usual? The deadline is tomorrow, as I'm sure most of you have forgotten."

Half a dozen surprised, unhappy faces stared back at her silently. "I thought so," DeeDee snapped. "I can't run this paper all by myself, you know. And if none of you thinks your work on the paper is important enough to make time for, then neither do I! You're all dismissed."

"What?" Kevin Hoffman asked.

"I said, *leave!*" DeeDee practically shouted. "All of you."

"Come on, DeeDee," Sasha said. "That's not fair. We always get everything done— eventually."

"I mean it," DeeDee said, her body rigid. "Everybody out of my office. Now!"

Slowly the *Record* staff collected their

things and shuffled out the door. Karen Jacobs was the last to leave. She paused beside DeeDee. "Is something wrong? Something besides the paper, I mean? I know it's none of my business, but if there's anything you want to talk about . . ."

DeeDee instantly felt remorse that she'd included Karen in her tirade. Karen was one of her best workers. She hadn't deserved to be yelled at.

"It's a long story," DeeDee said. "I'm sure you don't want to hear it."

"We could go to the Loft," Karen said. "Would you like that?"

DeeDee sighed. She wasn't really in the mood for one of the Loft's exotic milk shakes. But maybe talking about her problem would make her feel better.

"Okay," DeeDee said. "Thanks."

Half an hour later the two girls were sitting facing each other across a paint-splattered table, sipping thick, frosty shakes.

"So that's the story," DeeDee said as she finished giving Karen all the details. "I've never been so confused in my entire life. I mean, I've always tried to be a good daughter, and I've never let my parents down. But my father's going to hit the roof when I tell him I didn't get into Kingston."

"You mean, you didn't get in *yet*," Karen pointed out. "You're acting like they've rejected you. There's still a chance you'll get in later."

"But even if I did, now I'm not sure if I want to go," DeeDee said. "I guess what this all boils down to is that what I want to do with my life doesn't match what my father wants me to do."

Karen shook her head sympathetically. "I wish I had some words of wisdom to give you, but it's really something you have to work out on your own."

"I know," DeeDee said miserably. "I guess I'll have a lot to write about in my journal tonight."

"You know, DeeDee," Karen said slowly, "as long as you're writing about it in your journal, why not write it as an editorial for the *Record?* I'm sure there are a lot of kids who are going through the same kind of problem—like, how do you make your parents happy and make yourself happy, too?"

"That's a good idea," DeeDee said, "but I don't want to air my problems in front of the entire school."

"You wouldn't have to be too specific," Karen said. "You could just mention your situation as one example of how difficult it is to make a big decision when your parents want you to do something else."

For the first time that day DeeDee began to feel better. "It *would* be good to get it out of my system," she said. "You know, I'll do it!" She slapped her fist on the table.

She stood up and put some money on the table. "I'd better get going," she said. "I have a quiz to study for tonight, so I'll probably be up late writing the article. Want to take the bus with me?"

Before she could answer, Karen spotted Emily Van Patten sitting in a booth by herself, sipping on a jumbo-size malt and eating french fries. The willowy blond was staring into space, a troubled expression on her model-gorgeous face. This was the third time Karen had seen Emily pigging out lately. In fact, it looked as if Emily might have gained a few pounds. Her face, usually lean with high cheekbones, was definitely rounder. Maybe Emily was still depressed about Ben Newhouse.

Emily had dated Ben, Karen's new boyfriend, before she'd left River Heights to model and act in a television sitcom in New York City. Unfortunately, Emily had been written out of the show and had returned to River Heights to live with her father, who was separated from her mother. By then Ben had started dating Karen. For a while both girls had been miserable waiting for Ben to make up his mind about who he wanted to date. Finally they'd given him an ultimatum, and Ben had chosen Karen.

"You know what?" Karen said to DeeDee. "I see someone I want to talk to. I may stay a little longer."

"Okay," DeeDee said. "I'll see you tomorrow. And thanks for the moral support."

Karen paid for her shake and headed up the aisle to Emily's table. "Hi," she said. "What's up?"

Emily looked up glumly from her purple and pink swirled malt. "Nothing worth talking about," she said with a shrug.

Karen stared down at Emily with concern. "Look, Emily, I've shared a few junk food depressions with you, so don't try to kid me," she said.

Emily gave Karen a wan smile. "You caught me," she said. "Well, I've just been going through a hard time, that's all."

"I'm in my good-listener mode, if you want to talk," Karen said. "Want some company?"

Emily smiled. "Sure, that'd be great."

Karen slid into the booth across from Emily. "I guess it must be hard coming back to boring old River Heights after living in New York."

"No," Emily said, shaking her head. "It's nice to be back. I've just been thinking about my parents, actually. I never really thought about what it would mean when they split up." She sighed and stared back into her malt. "I just keep thinking that they might get back together, that I'll wake up and find out this whole divorce thing is a bad dream or something."

Karen nodded sympathetically. "It must be tough," she said. "If you ever want to talk about it, really talk, I mean, I'm willing to listen."

Emily studied Karen's face gratefully. "Thanks," she said. "I just may take you up on that."

9 ━━━⌁━

A beautiful young dark-haired woman, dressed in a white peasant blouse and jeans, sat on a tiny stage crooning a song in Spanish on her guitar. The stage was set up in a corner of South of the Border, where Lacey and Tom sat at a wooden table lit by the glow of a single votive candle.

"Isn't this romantic?" Lacey said, gazing dreamily across the table at Tom's handsome face.

Tom, his dark eyes shadowed in the dim light, didn't answer. Even in the near-dark, Lacey could see the tension in the set of his jaw.

"What's the matter?" Lacey asked. "This is supposed to be a celebration! Tomorrow night you're going to meet my parents. We won't have to hide from them anymore."

"From *them*," Tom said, his voice edgy. "But what about everyone else in school? What about my brother? Don't get me wrong, Lacey, I'm not Rick's biggest fan, but he's going to feel pretty stupid once the word gets out. And the longer we wait to tell him, the worse it's going to be."

"Why don't you two get along?" Lacey asked cautiously. "I'm not trying to change the subject or anything. I'm just curious, that's all."

Tom shrugged and leaned back in his chair. He wore a short-sleeved white T-shirt, and his bronzed, muscular arms gleamed even in the shadowy light. "Bad chemistry, I guess."

Lacey, her mouth burning from the spicy salsa she was eating, took a big gulp of water. "But it can't be as simple as that. You're brothers!"

"We're pretty different, though," Tom said. "Rick's more mainstream, I guess. And he was always jealous that I was bigger and stronger than he was."

"But you're older," Lacey said. "You had a head start."

"Try telling Rick that." Tom snorted. "Frankly, I couldn't care less which one of us has more muscles. All I want is to be left in peace so I can play my guitar. But for Rick, it's become an obsession. He could win a Mr. Universe pageant and still feel like a skinny weakling inside."

"I think you're right," Lacey said. "That may be the reason I've been so chicken about telling him. How's he going to feel if his older brother has beaten him out again?"

"It's something he'll have to face," Tom said. "But it's been hard on me, too. You and I are still passing each other in the halls, pretending we don't know each other. This isn't a spy flick, Lacey. We've got to get this thing out in the open."

"You're right," Lacey said, watching as a busboy hovered briefly near their table to refill their water glasses. "What we're doing isn't fair to any of us."

"Would it make it easier if I was with you when you told Rick?" Tom asked gently.

"No," Lacey said, her voice just above a whisper. "I think that might make it even worse for Rick. This is something I have to do alone. I just need a little more time to figure out exactly what I'm going to say."

Tom's dark green eyes reflected his impatience. "Okay," he said, his mouth set in a grim line. "But I don't know how much longer I can take this."

*   *   *

Thursday morning Brittany stepped off her schoolbus and right into Martin Ives.

"Good morning, Britty," Martin said cheerfully. His hair color had changed since the day before. Now it spanned several shades in the purple family.

"Love your hair," Brittany jeered.

Martin led her along the sidewalk. "There's no rule that says hair has to be black or brown or blond," he said easily.

Brittany rolled her eyes. "Look, Martin, I said I'd go to the basketball game with you, but I don't have to listen to you make excuses for how weird you are."

"What's so weird about me?" Martin demanded as they stepped onto the quad. "That I don't want to dress and think and be like everybody else?"

"That's a start," Brittany said.

Martin's black eyes smoldered. "I'm disappointed in you, Brittany," he said. "I thought you'd understand me better than that by now."

"I don't know what you're talking about," Brittany said irritably. She wasn't even listening to Martin anymore. She was too tired. Chip had called her half a dozen times the night before. The last call was at midnight. He hadn't come right out and asked if she was dating anybody else, but she knew that he suspected something.

Brittany had been very surprised — no, shocked — that Chip had sounded jealous. Usually he acted as if Brittany should feel lucky to go out with him.

Once, Brittany might have been happy to discover Chip was jealous, but now his childish behavior only added to her misery.

As Brittany and Martin headed toward the building, Brittany thought she saw someone watching them from behind a tree. It was only for an instant, but she had the very clear impression of a pair of Ray-Ban sunglasses peering out from under a navy blue hood.

"Did you see that?" Brittany asked Martin.

"See what?"

Before she could answer, Brittany saw the guy again. He was wearing jeans and a denim jacket with a hooded sweatshirt underneath. The hood and the dark sunglasses almost completely hid his face. There was something familiar about him, nonetheless.

"Let's go inside now," Brittany said, starting to get nervous.

"Why?" Martin asked. "What's wrong?"

"Don't ask questions," Brittany said, practically dragging Martin toward the front entrance.

But it was too late. Before Brittany could seek refuge inside the school, the hooded figure peered out again from behind the tree.

He lowered his sunglasses for a second, but it was long enough for Brittany to figure out what was going on. Chip Worthington was spying on her!

"I feel really sick," Brittany said honestly, breaking away from Martin. "I've got to go to the nurse's office."

Martin didn't try to stop her. After racing up the stairs, Brittany ran inside the building and down a hall, which was jammed with students. Hoping to lose herself in all the people, Brittany plunged into the crowd.

There were still ten minutes left before the final bell. Brittany darted past open classroom doors, hoping to find somewhere to be alone, at least until homeroom. Then, peering straight down the hall, she couldn't believe what she saw. It was Chip—still in his disguise, still looking for her.

What was he doing there? Brittany felt like screaming. She couldn't take the tension anymore.

Turning around, Brittany ran back the other way, darting from one side of the hall to the other. At last she reached a familiar, empty hallway. The door to the *Record* office was open at the end of it. With her last bit of strength, Brittany darted inside the office and shut the door behind her.

"Your editorial is amazing, DeeDee!" Karen Jacobs had been saying as she skimmed the pages in her hand. DeeDee was standing behind her, looking over Karen's shoulder.

As Brittany burst in, both girls turned toward the door. Brittany knew she was a mess, sweating, with her usually sleek dark hair now in a jumble around her face. She tried to assume a carefree expression.

"Hi!" she said casually, tucking her red silk blouse into her gray wool skirt, which had somehow twisted itself halfway around her body.

"Is anything wrong?" DeeDee asked, frowning.

"Wrong? No, of course not!" Brittany said, surreptitiously peering out through the glass on the office door to see if Chip had followed her.

DeeDee shrugged, then turned back to Karen. "I really have to thank you," she said. "I feel so much better since I wrote everything down, and I owe it all to you."

Karen smiled up at DeeDee, her hazel eyes glowing from the praise. Brittany fought back angry tears. After all she'd been through the past couple of days, this was the last thing she needed to see—Karen Jacobs winning over DeeDee Smith.

Brittany wanted to murder Martin Ives. Whatever she'd done to that nerdy jerk couldn't have been half as bad as the way he was destroying her life now.

The day had barely started, and already it was the worst day of Brittany's life.

"Okay, this is it," Lacey told herself as she stood in the doorway of the cafeteria. She couldn't avoid Rick any longer. It was time to tell him the truth.

Lacey stared across the rows of tables to where Rick was sitting alone. Nikki, Tim, Robin, and Calvin were still at their lockers. This was Lacey's chance to speak to Rick.

Lacey's legs felt as heavy as lead as she crossed the linoleum floor. A tremendous weight was pressing in on her chest, making it difficult for Lacey to take a deep breath.

"Hi, Rick," Lacey said softly as their eyes met.

Rick smiled at her for the first time in days. "Hello, Lacey," he said, his hazel eyes warm. "I haven't seen you around lately."

That's because I've been avoiding you, Lacey answered silently, but she did manage to smile back.

"That's a pretty racy jacket," Rick said. "My brother Tom has one just like it."

Here was a perfect opening. Lacey could say it *was* Tom's jacket, and he'd given it to her because they . . .

"Sit down," Rick said, patting the bench beside him. "It's been a long time since we've talked."

What was this nice act he was pulling? Maybe Rick had already found out about Tom and her and was just putting her off her guard before he started yelling.

"What did you want to talk about?" Lacey asked cautiously.

Rick shrugged. "I was just wondering how you're doing," he said. "And feeling a little guilty."

"Guilty?"

"Well, you know, about Katie and me. Ever since you caught us together last Friday, I've wanted to apologize for the way I avoided you and lied to you. You didn't deserve that, especially after the way you supported me when I was in the hospital."

Lacey felt a lump rise in her throat, and her eyes, dry from day after day of crying, began to tear once again. Lacey was surprised at her own reaction. She'd thought her feelings for Rick were dead. Or maybe it was just relief that Rick was finally saying the words she'd waited so long to hear.

"That's nice of you to say, Rick," Lacey said.

"I'm just sorry I wasn't nicer to you all along," Rick answered. He finished a last gulp of orange juice and tossed the container into a nearby trash can. "Even if I felt like things were over between us, I could have handled it better. I've learned an awful lot from this. I'm just sorry you were my guinea pig when I learned how *not* to end a relationship."

Lacey listened silently, her mind whirring, trying to figure out a way to bring up Tom. Then Rick stood up from the table. Where was he going? She hadn't said anything yet!

Lacey stood up, too, determined to follow him, but to her surprise, he didn't walk away. He just opened his arms to give her a hug. Lacey approached him reluctantly, unsure how she'd react when she felt his arms around her again.

"The worst thing," Rick whispered into her hair, "was that I started seeing someone behind your back. That was sneaky and underhanded, and I don't blame you if you never forgive me. I know you'd never do anything like that to me."

Lacey felt her stomach muscles clench. Of all the things Rick had ever said to her, this was the worst. Now she was cornered. She couldn't possibly tell Rick about Tom now. She had allowed him to feel guilty about Katie, but she was as guilty as he was now.

Lacey pulled back from Rick's embrace and almost died when she saw Tom standing a few feet behind Rick. The expression on Tom's face was a mixture of confusion, hurt, and anger. Instantly Lacey knew what Tom was thinking. He was afraid she and Rick had made up and were getting back together. Lacey was dying to run over to him and explain, but that would be giving everything away.

"Hey, Tom," Rick said casually, as if he were greeting a casual acquaintance, not his brother. "You remember Lacey, don't you?"

"How do I look?" Lacey asked her mother a few hours later in the dining room at their house. Lacey wore a white silk blouse with a shawl collar, onto which she'd pinned her grandmother's cameo pin, and a slim black skirt which ended just above her knees. The outfit was conservative, she knew, and she'd chosen it on purpose. She didn't want her parents to think her relationship with Tom was changing her too much.

Mrs. Dupree, kneeling in front of the marble-topped sideboard, turned and peered at Lacey through her horn-rimmed glasses. "You look very nice," she said, rising with two white candles in her hand. She placed them in the crystal candlesticks on the white linen tablecloth. "Is everything all set with Tom?"

Lacey sighed as she joined her mother at the dining room table and started setting the china dishes that were stacked at one end. After her encounter with Rick in the cafeteria that afternoon, she'd been afraid Tom would never speak to her again, let alone show up for dinner. Tom had beat it out of the lunchroom so fast that Lacey had thought she'd never find him.

She caught up with him outside, just as he was getting on his motorcycle. It had taken time, but Lacey finally convinced him there was no reason to be jealous of Rick.

Of course, she'd had to confess that she still hadn't told Rick the truth about Tom.

"Tom will be here at six o'clock," Lacey said, circling the snowy white table and setting down the gleaming plates. "I hope you and Dad are going to be nice to him."

"Of course we'll be nice. He's your guest."

"I'm always nice!" said a loud, cheerful voice. Robert Dupree appeared in the doorway of the dining room, wearing a navy blue blazer, khaki trousers, and an open-necked, white button-down shirt. He was a portly man with a slight double chin, but his face was handsome and healthy looking. His blond hair was straight and short and parted on the side. "Is he here yet?" Mr. Dupree asked.

"Not yet, Dad," Lacey said, glancing at her watch. It was almost six o'clock.

"I hope he's not late," Mr. Dupree said, strolling over to the sideboard to pluck a few grapes from a fruit bowl. "I'm starving!"

Just then Lacey heard the roar of an engine in the distance. The roar grew louder and louder as it approached, causing the crystal water glasses on the table to rattle.

"What on earth is that?" Mrs. Dupree rushed to the window, closely followed by her husband. They peered through the lace curtains covering the dining room window.

"Uh-oh," Mr. Dupree said, his usual good humor draining from his voice. "Looks like James Dean has come back from the grave."

Mrs. Dupree's alarm showed on her face. "Is he from one of those—biker gangs?"

"Would you please relax?" Lacey begged her parents. "Tom's just a nice guy who drives a motorcycle and wears a leather jacket. Don't judge him till you meet him, okay?"

Mr. and Mrs. Dupree turned away from the window to stare at Lacey. Before anyone could say more, the doorbell chimed.

"I'll get it," Lacey said. "Now remember —you promised to be nice."

Mrs. Dupree shrugged. "I'll just remember that he's Rick's brother."

Mr. Dupree stuffed his hands into his pockets and frowned.

Lacey ran to the door and pulled it open. Tom stood on the doorstep, his dark hair curling at the nape of his neck. He smiled at Lacey and pulled a wilted rose from inside his black leather jacket.

"For you," he said.

Lacey took the rose and propped it up so she could smell it. "Thanks," she said, taking his hand and pulling him into the front hall.

"Uh . . ." Tom looked down at his heavy black boots. "Wait a minute." He reached into his back pockets and pulled out a pair of loafers. "They're kind of crushed," he said apologetically, kicking off his boots, "but I figured I was meeting your parents, so . . ." Tom dropped his loafers to the floor and stepped into them.

Lacey smiled at Tom's thoughtfulness. Then she noticed that he wasn't wearing his usual jeans and black T-shirt, either. Instead, he had on a gray, long-sleeved shirt with black stripes, and a pair of black pants.

"You look nice," Lacey said, leaning forward to kiss him.

"Well, well, well," Mr. Dupree said heartily, breaking up the kiss as he came into the hall. "So this is your new young man!"

Lacey rolled her eyes at her father, hoping he'd get the hint to cut down on the jovial routine.

"We've been looking forward to meeting you," Mrs. Dupree said, extending her hand to Tom. "I guess this means we've met *all* the Stratton boys, right?"

Lacey shuddered inside. "Why don't we all sit down?" Lacey said quickly. "I know Dad's hungry, and I am, too."

The four of them moved inside and sat down at the long dining room table.

"So, Tom," Mrs. Dupree said brightly after they had all helped themselves to roast beef, mashed potatoes, and string beans. "Tell us about yourself."

Tom looked at Lacey questioningly. She knew he hated to talk about himself.

"Tom's a musician," Lacey prompted. "He's in a band, and he even writes some of his own songs."

"Is that right?" Mrs. Dupree asked, genuinely interested. "What kind of musical training have you had?"

Tom became noticeably uncomfortable. "Well, actually, I sort of taught myself."

"So you don't read music?" Mrs. Dupree asked, sounding disappointed.

"Not very well," Tom admitted. "I'm working on it, though. Right now, I'm spending more time writing lyrics."

Mrs. Dupree perked up at that. "You're a lyricist also? What kinds of songs do you write?"

Tom looked down at his hands, as if the answer were written there. "Well, let's see, there's 'Breaking the Speed Limit,' 'Fast Food, Fast Love,' 'Motorcycle Girl . . .'"

"This roast beef is delicious!" Lacey exclaimed, seeing the horror growing on her parents' faces. It was time to change the subject. "Have I mentioned how well my job at Platters is going?" Lacey worked part-time at a record store at the mall. "Maybe I should ask Lenny for another raise soon."

The ploy didn't work. Mr. Dupree kept his eyes locked on Tom. "Tell me, Tom," he said, "do you have an after-school job? I think it's very important that young people learn responsibility early on."

Tom nodded. "I work at Tony's Garage," he said. "I'm a mechanic."

"I can respect that," Mr. Dupree said. "I'm pretty good with machines myself. But I guess you're just doing it to earn extra money for college, right?"

Tom shrugged. "I'm not sure I'm going to college," he said. "Not right away, at least." He grinned at Lacey.

Mr. and Mrs. Dupree's mouths fell open. For Lacey's parents, going to college was not only expected, it was required. Choosing not to go was like choosing a life of crime.

This dinner was turning into a disaster. Lacey didn't know what she could possibly say to ease the tense silence that filled the room. "Pass the string beans, please," she asked weakly.

"You look beat!" Toby commented as he and DeeDee drove away from the Smiths' house Thursday evening. "I hope you're not too tired to go out tonight."

"I was about to say the same thing to you," DeeDee said.

"The coach *has* been driving us pretty hard," Toby admitted. "Why are *you* so tired?"

DeeDee sighed. "Nerves, I guess. I was up late last night, writing an editorial and studying. Then I couldn't fall asleep. I'm worried about how I'm going to tell my dad about Kingston. Don't say anything," DeeDee added quickly. "I promise I'm going to tell him tonight when I get home."

Toby reached for DeeDee's hand and squeezed it. "When you're ready, you'll tell him."

"Thanks for not getting on my case," DeeDee said as Toby turned onto a road lined with minimalls, fast-food restaurants, and car dealerships. "So, where are we going tonight? You were awfully secretive on the phone."

"You'll see," Toby said mysteriously as he made another turn onto a side road. The road was not well lit, but up ahead DeeDee saw a long line of cars, their red taillights glowing in the darkness. Toby pulled up to the end of the line.

"What is this?" DeeDee asked as the line of cars inched forward.

"Be patient," Toby said. Eventually, they reached a small wooden shack. Toby handed the man inside some money, and they pulled forward into a parking lot.

"What—?" DeeDee started to ask again, but then she saw the huge white screen towering over hundreds of parked cars. Next to each car was a pole with a speaker on it. "A drive-in movie!" DeeDee squealed. "I've never been to one before!"

"Then it's about time," Toby declared as he angled the car into an empty space. He reached outside for the speaker, which he hooked over the top of the window. He rolled the window as far up as he could to keep out the cold air.

"Now, I know what you're thinking," Toby said, facing DeeDee with a smile. "It's awfully cold to be sitting at a drive-in without a heater on. But I've come prepared."

Reaching into the back seat, Toby produced a blanket and a thermos. "Hot chocolate from the Westmoor Café," he said. "I noticed how much you like it. And if we huddle together, we should be able to keep each other warm."

Though DeeDee was thrilled at the thought of being so close to Toby, she was also a little nervous. What might a college guy expect from her? "I hope you don't think—" she ventured, but Toby cut her off.

"Of course not!" he said. "I hardly know you. I'm not going to let you take advantage of me."

DeeDee laughed. "I respect you too much," she told him.

"Good," Toby said. "Now, as long as that's settled, I think it's time for some hot chocolate." He opened the thermos and poured out a cupful for DeeDee. Steam from the cup rose into the cold air.

"Thanks," said DeeDee, taking the cup. "By the way, what are we seeing?"

"It's a double feature," Toby said. "I figured we could stay for just the first one and go out for a bite afterward. The first movie is *The Spider from Outer Space Who Ate Tokyo.* You said you liked science fiction."

DeeDee groaned. "It's a spoof, right?"

Toby shook his head. "Nope. It's a real, authentic, 1955 Japanese bug movie. Think of it as a historical artifact."

DeeDee giggled as the huge screen in front of them lit up with numbers counting down from ten to one. The speaker to Toby's left crackled with static. Then, as the credits rolled against a plain black background, the speaker played tinny, melodramatic music.

The two of them cuddled under the blanket as a flying saucer landed on Earth and a giant spider crawled out of it. The movie, originally in Japanese, had been dubbed into English, but the characters spoke very quickly, and it was hard to understand what they were saying. The spider crawled to Tokyo and wove webs between buildings, in which planes and helicopters got stuck while people ran around screaming.

The movie was funny, but DeeDee felt her eyelids drooping. She hadn't slept the night before, and now she felt very relaxed. The last thing DeeDee remembered before she fell asleep was a young woman taking a bubble bath while one of the spider's tentacles reached in through the bathroom window to grab her.

11

The silence was deafening. For the past five minutes Lacey's parents hadn't said a word to Tom or to her. They just stared at Tom as they chewed, their eyes plainly disapproving.

"Have I mentioned how well I'm doing at Platters?" Lacey asked for the third time.

Tom pushed his chair back from the table, his plate still half-filled with food. "Thanks for dinner. It was great. I've got to be going," he mumbled.

"But, Rick!" Mrs. Dupree exclaimed. "You haven't finished eating."

Lacey stared at her mother in horror.

"Oh, I'm terribly sorry," Mrs. Dupree said quickly. "I meant Tom, of course."

"How *is* Rick?" Mr. Dupree asked.

"He's fine," Tom said, rising to his feet. "Thanks again for dinner," he said. "It was delicious."

"Do you really have to go, Tom?" Lacey asked, jumping up out of her chair. "There's apple pie for dessert."

"Sorry. I've got band rehearsal," Tom said. "Nice meeting you, Mr. and Mrs. Dupree."

Barely able to contain her fury at her parents, Lacey followed Tom out to the front hall. It was only seven o'clock. Tom had plenty of time to get to his eight o'clock rehearsal, but her parents had driven him away.

Lacey opened the hall closet and handed Tom his leather jacket. Then she threw on her wool coat. "I'll go with you," she said.

The air was still and cold as Lacey walked Tom to his motorcycle. "I'm sorry," Lacey said, her breath coming out in puffy clouds. "I didn't realize my parents would be such jerks."

"They're not jerks," Tom said. "They're just parents, asking parent-type questions."

"But I wanted you to like them," Lacey said. "I still do. I hope you'll give them another chance."

Tom gave her a lopsided grin and wrapped

his arms around her waist. "I hope they'll give *me* another chance."

Lacey pressed her cheek against the cool leather of Tom's jacket. "It shouldn't matter what they think," she said. "It shouldn't matter what anyone thinks. This is between you and me and no one else." She sighed. "So why is everything such a mess?"

Tom hugged her, hard. "We're not living on a desert island," he said. "And where there are people, there are hurt feelings."

Lacey raised her face to Tom's. He bent his head down toward her, and Lacey closed her eyes.

"Uh-oh," Tom said just before their lips touched. "I think your parents are calling you."

Lacey opened her eyes and saw the dining room light in her house flashing off and on. "I can't believe this!" she said indignantly. "They're trying to destroy my life!"

"I'd better get going," Tom said, reaching for his helmet. "By the way, do you want to go to the Westmoor basketball game with me on Saturday?"

Of course she wanted to go. But what if Rick was there? Rick would see them together. On the other hand, there was no reason not to break the news to Rick before Saturday. No reason except her lack of courage.

"I'd love to," Lacey said. There. She'd done it. Now she'd have to tell Rick the next day. The dining room light flicked on and off again. "I'll see you tomorrow." Lacey gave Tom a quick kiss on the cheek and raced back inside as Tom's motorcycle roared off.

Her parents were waiting in the front hall, Mrs. Dupree clutching her linen napkin.

"Was that really necessary?" Lacey asked hotly. "It's bad enough you were rude to Tom, but did you have to act like the River Heights police? We were just saying good-bye."

"*We* were rude?" Mrs. Dupree exclaimed. "We tried our very best to be nice to that boy."

"Rick was never like that," Mr. Dupree said. "When you ask Rick a question, he gives you a whole sentence for an answer. He smiles once in a while, too. It's hard to believe he and Tom come from the same family."

"Stop comparing him to Rick!" Lacey shouted. "You're not being fair to Tom or to me. I suppose the next thing you're going to say is that you don't want me to see him because he wears a leather jacket."

"No," Mrs. Dupree began. "We're not saying that—"

"Good," Lacey said, taking off her coat and flinging it into the closet. "Because I'm going to keep seeing him whether you like it or not!"

Tap! Tap! Tap! The knocking came from outside DeeDee's window. The old man they'd paid to get in was waving at her and mouthing something. DeeDee rolled down her window.

"Closing time, young lady," he said.

DeeDee looked at the old man sheepishly. "Sorry," she said. "I guess we fell asleep."

"You're not the only ones," the old man said, pointing to a few other cars in the nearly empty lot.

"Thanks," DeeDee said. She shook Toby gently.

Toby stirred. "Just five more minutes, Mom."

"I'm not your mom," DeeDee told him.

At that Toby opened his eyes. "Oh, no!" he said when he realized what had happened. "What time is it?"

DeeDee pushed her coat sleeve out of the way to read the glowing green numbers on her watch. She gasped in horror. "It's almost one o'clock! That's two hours past my curfew. My parents are going to kill me."

Without another word Toby started the car and zoomed out of the lot. "I'm really sorry," he said. "I don't know what happened."

DeeDee tried not to let Toby know how

scared she was of what her parents' reaction would be. "It's not your fault," she said. "We were both tired, and we fell asleep."

"I'll go in with you and explain what happened," Toby said. "Otherwise, they may never let me see you again."

"They may not even if you *do* try to explain," DeeDee said grimly as they passed a Buddy Burger, Cluck Cluck Chicken, and the Doughnut Hole. "In fact, I think it would probably be safer if you *didn't* come in. You may be bigger than my dad, but he'll be a lot madder."

Toby drove into DeeDee's neighborhood, then turned onto her street. Up ahead, the yellow light was on by the Smiths' front door, but the rest of the house was dark.

"Maybe they're asleep," Toby said as he pulled up in front of DeeDee's house.

"Let's hope so," DeeDee said, kissing him on the cheek. "I'll see you Saturday. If I'm not grounded, that is."

"I'll call you tomorrow," Toby promised.

As Toby pulled away from the house, DeeDee hurried up the front walk. Maybe her parents *were* asleep. If she could just let herself into the house quietly, maybe they'd never know how late she'd come home.

Pausing under the yellow light, DeeDee fished around in her crowded purse for her house key. It was in there somewhere, but she had so many things in her purse. Where was her key?

DeeDee was so busy fumbling in her purse that she never heard the front door open. And she didn't notice when the letter from Kingston fell out of her purse, gently fluttered through the winter air, and landed on the tops of her father's bedroom slippers.

"Ahhhhem!" Mr. Smith cleared his throat.

DeeDee froze. Only her eyes rolled upward to see her father towering above her, big and bulky in his maroon velour bathrobe. Without a word he stooped down, picked up the folded piece of white paper, and scanned it quickly. The scowl on his face flickered for an instant, then returned.

"Where have you been? And what have you been doing in the middle of the night with that jock? Do you think I don't know what goes on with boys in the back seats of cars?"

"Dad!" DeeDee protested. "We didn't do anything. We just fell asleep——"

"Fell asleep?" Mr. Smith yelled. "Where were you that you could fall asleep? I'll kill him!"

"Dad! Dad! You've got it all wrong!" DeeDee shouted. "We went to a drive-in."

"That's it!" Mr. Smith yelled, taking hold of DeeDee's arm and pulling her into the house. "You're grounded. And you're never to see that young man again."

"But I told you the truth!" DeeDee insisted. "Don't you trust me?"

"Trust you?" Mr. Smith roared, holding up the letter from Kingston. "After you kept this from me? After you lied and said it never arrived?"

"I was planning to tell you," DeeDee began, but her father held up his hand.

"Exactly how long were you planning to keep this from me?" he demanded. "Or were you going to let me drive you all the way to Kingston and tell me then?"

"Maybe I just didn't know how to tell you I didn't get in!" DeeDee cried, clutching her purse against her. "Maybe I was so worried about disappointing you that I was afraid to say anything."

"Excuses, excuses," Mr. Smith said.

DeeDee could understand why her dad was upset. She'd never come home so late before, and she'd never hidden anything from him, but he had no right to treat her like this.

"Okay," DeeDee said, gritting her teeth. "You want to know why I didn't tell you about Kingston? It's because I *hate* that school! Even if they *do* accept me, I won't go there!"

Pushing past her father, DeeDee ran up the stairs to her room and slammed the door. Then she fell onto her bed and burst into tears.

12 ⟴

Friday afternoon Lacey sat alone in the bleachers, watching the wiry, muscular boys grappling on the mats below her. The River Heights High wrestling team was having a practice, and Rick was with them.

Even though Lacey had come to tell Rick, once and for all, that she was seeing his brother, she couldn't help feeling slightly attracted to him still. But that didn't matter anymore. What mattered was clearing the way so she and Tom could be together.

The wrestling coach blew his whistle, and the boys grabbed their towels and started heading for the locker room. Lacey had to catch Rick before he disappeared.

"Rick!" she called, clambering down the wooden bleachers.

Rick turned and gave her a curious half-smile. "I thought you weren't interested in wrestling," he said as she drew near.

"I need to talk to you," Lacey said. "It's very important."

Rick shrugged. "Sure," he said. "Coach wants to see me in his office, but I can take a minute." He sat down on the bottom row of bleachers and Lacey sat beside him. "What's up?" he asked.

Now that Lacey finally had Rick's full attention, she didn't know how to begin. "This is kind of difficult to say," she said, "and I'm not sure you'll want to hear this, but . . ."

Rick didn't interrupt. He just looked at her patiently.

"Okay," Lacey began again. "When you were so nice to me yesterday and said all those sweet things, it made it hard for me to admit that I'm—"

"Wait a minute," Rick said, holding up his hand. "I think I see what you're getting at."

"You do?" Lacey asked, surprised.

Rick leaned forward and rested his elbows on his knees. "I think you got the wrong idea yesterday," he said, looking down at the floor. "I know I was a lot nicer to you than I have been in a while, but that doesn't mean I want us to get back together. If I did anything to lead you on, I'm sorry. You're still a great person, Lacey, but I'm seeing Katie now. It's over between us. I'm sorry."

"But you don't understand!" Lacey pleaded. "That's not what I—"

"Stratton!" thundered a loud, male voice from the opposite side of the gym.

"Sorry, Lacey," Rick said, hopping to his feet. "That's the coach. I told you he wants to see me."

"But I haven't said—"

"Stratton! Now!" ordered the coach.

"See ya," Rick said, waving as he sprinted away.

Lacey kicked the back of her shoes against the bleacher in frustration. She was right back where she started. Tom was going to be furious with her, and there was no way she could go to the Westmoor game with him now. Even though Rick was a sneak and saw someone behind her back, Lacey just couldn't be. Especially not with Rick's brother.

Slinging her knapsack over one shoulder, Lacey left the gym. Why was everything going so wrong in her life? She was trying to be honest with Rick, but Tom would think she was playing games. Her parents, while they hadn't forbidden her to see Tom again, clearly didn't like him. And now, at the end of the hall, she saw Nikki and Robin.

"Lacey!" Nikki called, waving. Her blond hair was pulled back with a tan headband that matched her tan parka.

Lacey approached cautiously, keeping her eyes on Robin. Robin was wearing a white oversize sweatshirt with big black polka dots, and black tights, black- and white-striped socks, and black hightop sneakers. Her knapsack had a black and white checkerboard pattern. Even her puffy down jacket was black.

Lacey tried to read Robin's expression as she approached. Robin didn't look as mad as she had a few days earlier.

"Hi," Lacey said tentatively.

Nikki said hi, and Robin gave Lacey a little smile.

"You might not want to smile at me once I tell you what happened just now," Lacey said. She explained how she'd tried and failed, once again, to tell Rick about Tom.

To Lacey's great relief, Robin patted her on the shoulder. "At least you tried," Robin said. "I've been doing some serious thinking. Or, rather," she said, correcting herself, "I've been listening to Nikki the Peacemaker here, and I've realized how selfish I've been lately. I was so afraid of the way you've changed that I haven't stopped to think how *you* must be feeling right now."

"Well," Lacey said, "I *do* feel different sometimes. But I'm still your friend. That won't change."

"I wouldn't blame you if you *weren't* my friend anymore," Robin said guiltily. "Here you've been going through a tough time, and I haven't supported you at all."

"You had a right to be angry," Lacey said.

"I guess some of it has to do with Calvin, too," Robin went on. "He's so bummed that our happy group is breaking up that it rubbed off on me."

"But we can't expect things to stay the same forever," Lacey added.

"Speaking of new developments," Nikki broke in, "how was dinner last night with Tom and your parents?"

Lacey sighed. "It was a total disaster. I'd rather not talk about it right now, if you don't mind."

"Are you and Tom going to the basketball game tomorrow?" Nikki asked. "We're all going to the Pizza Palace afterward."

Lacey shook her head. "It sounds like fun, but I can't go to the game with Tom now. Rick is bound to be there with Katie. We can't risk running into him before I tell Rick about us."

"Calvin told me Rick isn't going to the game. He feels bad about the way he treated you, and he doesn't want to rub it in by showing up with Katie."

"He really *must* feel bad," Lacey said. "He's been acting so nice to me lately."

The three girls emerged into the weak sunlight and walked down the stairs of the north wing. A few fluffy clouds scudded across an otherwise clear sky, and birds twittered from the empty branches of the trees lining the walkway.

"Does anyone need a ride home?" Lacey asked as they neared the student parking lot.

"Thanks, but I have my car," Nikki said.

"Calvin's meeting me here in a few minutes," Robin added. "I'm glad we got a chance to talk, though."

"Me, too," Lacey said.

Robin scuffed her black hightops along the pavement. "Well, see ya, I guess."

"Yeah. See ya." Lacey gave Nikki and Robin a quick smile and headed for her car. She still felt a little uncomfortable with Robin, but at least they were speaking. That was something to be happy about.

Lacey let herself into the bright yellow Buick and sat behind the steering wheel for a moment, waiting for the engine and the heater to warm up. There might be something else to be happy about, she suddenly realized.

Robin had said Rick wouldn't be going to

the game. That meant she and Tom could go after all! They could sit on the Westmoor side, where no one from school would see them. That way they'd be safe from prying eyes and blabbing mouths. Rick would never even know they'd been there.

Lacey grinned as she shifted the car into reverse and backed out of her parking space, narrowly clearing Jeremy Pratt's Porsche. It was amazing how two of her problems had been solved in such a short time. Saturday was going to be great, Lacey could just feel it.

By the time DeeDee left school on Friday, it was almost dark. DeeDee and Karen had stayed late, overseeing the paste-up of next week's paper. After DeeDee had blown up at the meeting, all the staff had turned in their articles on time.

DeeDee felt bad that she'd taken her frustrations out on her staff. That was totally unprofessional. But it wouldn't happen again, because DeeDee was about to resolve her Kingston problem once and for all.

When DeeDee marched through the front door of her house, her parents were both home and sitting in the living room.

"Hi, honey," Mrs. Smith said pleasantly when DeeDee entered.

Mr. Smith said nothing. He stared straight ahead, as if he didn't see DeeDee. DeeDee couldn't remember when she'd ever seen him this angry, but she was angry, too.

"Dad," she said quietly, "I think it's time we talked."

Mr. Smith spoke without turning his head. "I have nothing to say to you."

"Please, Harold," Mrs. Smith said, putting her needlepoint aside. "You can't go on like this forever."

"My daughter has betrayed me," Mr. Smith said, speaking as if DeeDee weren't even in the room. "For seventeen years I've trusted her, put all my hopes into her, and look what she's done to me."

"What *I've* done to you?" DeeDee cried. "Did you ever, once, in the past seventeen years think about what I wanted? You've been so set on my following in your footsteps —going to Kingston, becoming a newspaper editor just like you. I've had no choice in the matter. And since I've always been such a good little girl, I never even *considered* doing anything but what you wanted me to do."

"Good little girl!" Mr. Smith snorted. "Good little girls don't show up on the doorstep two hours past their curfew after parking with some college guy."

"I told you, nothing happened," DeeDee said. "We just fell asleep."

"That's beside the point," her father said, turning his dark, flashing eyes toward her.

"The point is, you lied to me. You said you hadn't heard from Kingston when the letter was in your pocketbook all along."

"I'm sorry for that," DeeDee said. "But *you're* the reason I couldn't tell you. I knew how disappointed you'd be. I was trying to figure out some way to break it to you gently."

Mr. Smith picked up his magazine and pretended to read it.

"Dad!" DeeDee exclaimed. "Listen to me! I know I didn't handle this the best way that I could, but you were putting so much pressure on me! You've been acting like Kingston is the only school in the universe. But there are other schools, *better* schools for what I want to do."

Mr. Smith looked up sharply from his magazine. "What *do* you want?" he asked.

"I want to go into TV news, not print. I want to be on camera."

Mr. Smith was clearly astonished. "I thought you liked to write!"

"I do," DeeDee said, "but I want to go further. And I'd like to go to a school where I can get broadcast experience. A school like Westmoor. I've got my application all filled out."

"This is outrageous!" Mr. Smith cried, throwing down his magazine. "Do you mean to say that you not only hid that letter from me, but you've also been applying to another school behind my back? I thought I knew my own daughter, but obviously I was wrong."

DeeDee wanted to slam her fist right through the wall. It was clear she wasn't getting through to her father. "I should have known better than to think you'd under-stand!" she shouted. "It's obvious that the one thing you didn't learn at Kingston was to be open-minded!"

DeeDee stormed out of the living room and up the stairs. Why was it so difficult to explain to him? If only there was some way she could make her father see.

The editorial! That was it! The editorial she'd written for next week's paper. That explained her feelings better than anything she could tell him in person. She had a copy in her bag.

DeeDee turned right around and ran back down the stairs. Her father looked up when she charged back into the room.

"Here!" DeeDee said, shoving the copy into his hands. "Read this!"

13 ⌒⌒⌒

Brrrrrr. Brrrrrr.

Brittany listened as the phone rang on the other end of the line Saturday morning.

"Hello?" Chip answered.

Burrowing deeper under the covers on her bed, Brittany tried to summon up all her acting skills. "Hi, Chip," she said cheerfully. "It's me."

"Uh-huh," Chip said, without much enthusiasm. Maybe, Brittany thought, she should build him up a little before she told him about the change of plan for the Westmoor basketball game that afternoon.

"I've missed you," she said sweetly.

"I'll bet," Chip said dryly. "You've canceled on me twice this week."

"You know I didn't want to," Brittany said. "I've just had a lot of work to do at the *Record.*"

"I've been busy, too, but I still made time for you," Chip said.

Brittany stared at the receiver in disbelief. In all the time she'd been dating Chip, that was the closest he'd ever come to saying he cared about her. Usually all he did was brag about his father's sailboat and his mother's social connections and how he was sure to be accepted by every Ivy League school.

"Well, you're really organized," Brittany said, trying to placate him, "but I just panic when I get overloaded like this. And that's the reason I'm calling."

"Don't tell me," Chip said, his voice tense. "You can't go to the game with me this afternoon, right?"

"Don't be silly!" Brittany cooed. "You know how much I've been looking forward to this. There's just one teeny tiny change of plan."

"Uh-huh," Chip said.

"I'd like to meet you at the game, instead of having you pick me up," Brittany told him. "See, I have to work at my mom's flower shop after the game, and my dad's driving her there this morning so I can drive her car to the game and then get to work." Brittany spoke quickly, hoping he'd believe her.

There was silence on the other end of the line.

"Chip?" Brittany asked. "Are you still there?"

"Yeah, I'm here," Chip said. "So where do you want me to meet you?"

Brittany heaved a sigh of relief. Chip didn't sound happy, but at least he'd bought her story! "Why don't I meet you by the information booth at quarter to one?" she said.

The game started at one o'clock, and Brittany had already told Martin to pick her up at noon. That way they'd arrive at Westmoor and be seated by twelve-thirty. Then Brittany could make an excuse to leave Martin, find Chip, and make sure they sat as far away from Martin as possible.

Chip sighed on the other end of the phone. "Okay," he said. "See you there."

Brittany was taking a big risk, but the Westmoor stadium was huge, and thousands of people would be there. She'd just have to be careful. Very careful.

The sounds of squeaking sneakers and basketballs smacking the floor echoed in the cavernous Westmoor University Arena that afternoon.

Lacey had never been much of a basketball fan, but she couldn't help getting caught up in the excitement of the game. The score had been close from the beginning, and the lead kept changing every few minutes.

Lacey could tell Tom was excited, too. His forest green eyes barely blinked as he stared at the action down on the court, and whenever River Heights lost the ball, he'd shake a clenched fist.

"Isn't this great?" Lacey asked Tom, her eyes shining.

Tom nodded, not looking away from the court.

Lacey knew his interest in the game wasn't the only reason he wasn't saying much. Tom was still mad that Lacey hadn't told Rick yet.

The buzzer went off, signaling the end of the first quarter. Lacey and Tom stayed seated. They didn't dare go to the snack bar for fear someone they knew might see them.

"I want you to know something," Lacey said. She placed her hand over Tom's clenched fist, which rested on the faded denim knee of his jeans. "I'm just as sick of this sneaking around as you are. Tomorrow I'm going over to your house—I promise—and I'm telling Rick the truth, no matter what."

"I've heard that before," Tom said, looking everywhere but at her.

"Tom, look at me, please," Lacey begged. "I know I haven't handled this very well.

But that has nothing to do with my feelings for you. You mean so much to me, and pretty soon the whole world's going to know it.''

Tom said nothing.

Lacey took a deep breath. ''Tom,'' she said, ''if I can't find Rick tomorrow, then *you* can tell him. Okay? Then he'll definitely find out one way or another.''

Tom's eyes warmed slightly, and she saw a shadow of his lopsided grin. ''It's a good thing you said that,'' he said, ''because that's what I was going to do, anyway.''

He shifted over on the bleacher and put his arm around Lacey. ''For any other girl I'd never have put myself through this. But if it means we'll be together in the end, it's worth it.''

Lacey leaned her head against Tom's chest and sighed happily.

''I have an idea,'' Tom said. ''Why don't we go to the Pizza Palace after the game?''

Lacey felt a cold chill wash over her. It would be risky going to a popular River Heights High hangout. Someone would be sure to see them.

On the other hand, it was unlikely anyone would get to Rick before Lacey herself did, the next morning. And Tom could intercept any calls that night.

"Sure," Lacey said. "The Pizza Palace sounds great. We can practice being a normal couple."

Tom playfully ruffled Lacey's hair. "Watch it," he joked. "I never said I wanted to be normal."

"That's what I like about you," Lacey said, tilting her face up so she could study Tom's handsome profile. She didn't see much, though, because Tom immediately leaned over her and kissed her gently on the lips.

"I don't know why we have to sit way up here," Chip grumbled. "I can hardly see!"

Brittany, too, was uncomfortable on the hard wooden bleacher near the ceiling of the stadium. But she didn't care so much that she couldn't see. Basketball was a pointless game. On the court below them, skinny young men, with legs like stilts, ran back and forth like scrawny chickens, trying to get a ball through a hoop.

"There are lots of empty seats farther down," Chip said, pointing. "Let's move."

"No!" Brittany exclaimed. She'd chosen these seats very carefully. Martin was sitting on the opposite side of the stadium, near the middle. If she and Chip moved down, they'd be more visible to Martin, and vice versa. "I mean, it's more . . . *private* here." She lay her head on Chip's shoulder and smiled up at him prettily.

Chip seemed to relax a little. "It's not a bad game," he admitted. "Not that I really like to attend *public* school functions, but these teams are pretty good. That Westmoor guy, Jackson, is really racking up the points!"

Brittany nodded even though she didn't have the slightest idea who Jackson was. Then she checked her watch. She'd been with Chip for fifteen minutes. She'd told Martin she was going to the ladies' room. She had to get back to him before he started wandering around searching for her.

Brittany put a hand to her forehead and closed her eyes.

"What's wrong?" Chip asked.

Brittany opened her eyes and smiled weakly. "I didn't eat much breakfast this morning. I'm starting to feel a little dizzy."

Chip's eyes slid back to the game, then reluctantly to Brittany. "I'll get you something," he said, standing up. "What do you want?"

Brittany pulled him back down to the bench. "Oh, no," she said. "I couldn't possibly tear you away from the game. I know how much you're enjoying it. I'll just run down to the snack bar and get something. I'll be right back."

"You're sure?" Chip asked, already engrossed in the action down on the court.

"Positive," Brittany said, already sprinting down the stairs.

She raced through a long tunnel into the hallway circling the stadium.

Slowing her pace as she ran up a tunnel on the far side, Brittany smoothed her hair and caught her breath. She didn't want Martin to suspect she was up to anything. She caught Martin's eye and waved.

"Where have you been?" Martin asked irritably. That day his hair was black, brown, and yellow.

"You wouldn't believe how long the line was in the ladies' room," Brittany lied. "It's always like that, whenever you go to a public place."

"I thought you'd skipped out on me," Martin said suspiciously.

"You know I'd never do that, Martin," Brittany said innocently. "A deal's a deal."

"Tell me something, Brittany," Martin said slyly. "After all this time we've spent together, have your feelings about me changed at all?"

Uh-oh. Martin was getting that sappy look, just like the one he'd worn last year when he'd kept following her around. He couldn't still have a crush on her, could he?

"What do you mean?" Brittany asked cautiously.

"Well," Martin began, "I know you and I are very different people, but now that you know me a little better, do you think you could ever——"

But before Martin could finish his sentence, Brittany spotted Chip emerging from one of the long tunnels that led into the bleachers. He was far away, but she recognized his navy blue Talbot blazer.

Chip turned left and made his way across the aisle below Brittany. He was moving slowly, surveying the crowd. Brittany's heart stopped. She knew what Chip was doing. He was hunting her down!

14

"Go, Bears!" screamed Karen Jacobs, jumping up from her seat in the stands and cupping her hands around her mouth. She was wearing Ben Newhouse's varsity jacket with the sleeves rolled up. Ben sat on Karen's right, pounding his fists against his knees as he watched the game.

DeeDee, sitting on the other side of Karen, stared glumly at the packed arena. It seemed as if practically everyone in River Heights had shown up for the game.

The game was close, too, even though the college team was older, taller, and more experienced. River Heights had several excellent players and a great new coach.

The new coach, Tim Unruh, was an ex-military man. He was tough on the team, but in a few short weeks he'd whipped them into the best shape they'd ever been in.

DeeDee could barely pay attention even though Toby was down on the court right then, scoring every few minutes. All she could think about was that she and her father hadn't said a word to each other since the night before when she'd shoved her editorial into his hands. She'd gone up to her room right afterward and hadn't gone downstairs for dinner. That morning, when she got up, her father had already left to do some errands.

DeeDee's mother had said she could go to the game, even though her father had grounded her. Usually, her parents stuck together when it came to discipline. DeeDee didn't ask any questions but grabbed her coat and ran to Karen's house, where everyone was meeting to go to the game.

Ellen Ming, sitting to DeeDee's left, stood up as the River Heights team swiped the ball and raced down the court toward their basket. "You can do it!" she screamed, her silky black hair bouncing as she jumped up and down. "Show those old guys what we're made of!"

"You'd better not say that around Dee-Dee," joked Kevin Hoffman, Ellen's boyfriend.

"Sorry," Ellen said, but DeeDee was hardly listening. She was trying to decide whether she needed glasses. In the bleachers across the court she saw two people who looked very familiar.

DeeDee blinked and looked again, but the mirage persisted. The middle-aged couple —a slender, attractive woman and an overweight, balding man—looked exactly like DeeDee's parents!

DeeDee shook her head in disbelief, but just then her mother caught her eye and waved. DeeDee wasn't crazy, but what were they doing there? As DeeDee raised her hand in a halfhearted greeting, her mother pointed at something her father was holding in his hand.

DeeDee's mouth fell open in amazement. Her father was waving a Westmoor banner!

Chip was getting close. Brittany couldn't let him see her with Martin, but she knew Martin wouldn't let her leave his side. Brittany considered throwing herself to the floor, but then she came up with a better plan.

"Martin," she said, mustering all her charm, "you must have read my mind. I know we got together for—well, the wrong reasons, but my feelings for you *have* changed. I've seen a whole new side of you." Brittany wanted to gag at her own words. She sounded like a bad soap opera. But at this point she'd say anything to get him to do what she wanted. "Let's start all over again, as friends," Brittany finished.

Martin looked skeptical. "How?" he asked.

Chip was getting closer. Brittany had to do something fast! "You could start by getting me a soda," Brittany said, letting her hand rest lightly on Martin's bony shoulder.

"Okay," Martin said, getting up. "What kind do you want?"

"Diet anything," Brittany said. And hurry! she added to herself. Any second now Chip would glance up and see them.

"I'll be right back," Martin said. "But don't pull any funny stuff while I'm gone."

Brittany looked at Martin with total innocence.

As soon as Martin had disappeared, Brittany ducked down, pretending she'd dropped something.

When she peeked up a few minutes later, Chip was gone. Now was her chance to get back to her other seat. Brittany hurried down the aisle and ran back through a tunnel to the circular hallway. There were only a few people standing at the nearest snack bar, pumping mustard onto foot-long hotdogs. Martin must have gone to another refreshment stand.

Brittany was about to make a run for it when she saw something that stopped her dead. A middle-aged man and a younger woman were leaning against the snack bar, sharing a box of caramel-coated popcorn. They were laughing and feeding each other and seemed in no hurry to get back to the game.

The fascinating part was not so much *what* they were doing as *who* they were. The woman, her carrot red hair enveloping her head like a halo, was Roxy Muldoon, a new assistant drama teacher at River Heights High. The man, with graying hair and a lean build, was Emily Van Patten's father!

What a juicy piece of gossip for her column—a teacher and a student's father!

Of course, Brittany couldn't break the story right away. She'd have to get more facts and figure out an angle. Still, stumbling onto the story was the first good thing that had happened to her all day.

Brittany had to get going. She checked left, then right. No sign of Chip or Martin. Brittany continued on when she heard two different people call her name.

Brittany didn't know which way to turn. Before she could decide, she felt Martin's hand on her shoulder. Just in front of her was a gorgeous guy.

It wasn't Chip Worthington. It was her

ex-boyfriend, Westmoor freshman Jack Reilly! Brittany wanted to turn and run, but Martin was blocking her way.

Jack looked as fantastic as Brittany remembered. Tall and muscular, he was wearing a green polo sweater.

Whenever Brittany had fantasized about meeting Jack again, she'd planned to have a hunk on her arm, but it wasn't working out that way. All she had to show for herself was scrawny, pimply Martin Ives with his tricolor hair! This had to be the most embarrassing moment of her life.

Brittany felt Martin's fingers dig sharply into her upper arm. "I can't believe I almost fell for that let's-be-friends routine," he said. "I'll never trust you again."

Brittany felt her face grow hot with rage. "And *you,* Martin Ives—every moment I've spent with you has been sheer torture!"

"Good!" Martin shouted. "Because I'm not leaving your side the rest of the day."

"You're despicable!" Brittany cried, stamping her foot. Out of the corner of her eye she saw Jack pass by without even saying hello.

Karen tapped DeeDee on the shoulder. "Hey," she said, "aren't those your parents?"

"I see them," DeeDee said, still dazed,

"but I don't believe it. My father is set on my going to Kingston. So what's he doing here with a Westmoor banner?"

"Maybe he's had a change of heart," Ellen suggested.

"I doubt it," DeeDee said. "If there's anyone more stubborn than I am, it's him. Maybe my mother handcuffed him and dragged him here."

The buzzer went off, signaling the end of the second quarter. "I think your mom's waving to you," Karen said, pointing. "Aren't you going to go over and say hi?"

"Oh, right," DeeDee said, "and let my dad yell at me again? I came here to get away from him."

"He doesn't look angry to me," Ellen said.

DeeDee glanced at her parents again. Her father was sheepishly waving to her. What could all this mean? She couldn't just ignore them. "I'll meet you a little later, okay?" DeeDee said finally.

"Good luck!" Karen and Ellen called as DeeDee rose and edged past the people in her row.

As DeeDee waded through the crowd below, she thought she saw Rick Stratton holding hands with a petite, dark-haired girl. They were gazing into each other's eyes. DeeDee was confused. Wasn't Rick Stratton going with Lacey Dupree?

But DeeDee didn't have time to think about them. She wanted to reach her parents before the next quarter started and the noise and cheering got too loud to hear what they had to say. At last DeeDee reached her parents' row. They were sitting on the aisle, and they moved over to make room for her.

"Hi," DeeDee said shyly as she sat down.

"Hi," her mother said, giving her a peck on the cheek.

Mr. Smith gave DeeDee a weak smile.

"So what's going on?" DeeDee said. "Have you two suddenly taken an interest in basketball?"

"DeeDee," her mother scolded, "don't be hard on your father. It was difficult enough for him to come here today."

Mr. Smith reached into the pocket of his tan raincoat and pulled out DeeDee's editorial. "Nice piece of writing," he said.

"Thanks," DeeDee said, still perplexed.

Her father cleared his throat and stared up at the ceiling, as if searching for words up there. Then he focused back on DeeDee. "Your article made me think long and hard," he said finally. "It gave me more insight into how you really feel about this whole Kingston thing. I never knew you had such mixed feelings. Why didn't you say something earlier?"

"I hardly knew myself," DeeDee said. "I

felt as if I had to go to Kingston because *you* went there.''

Mr. Smith rolled the typewritten pages into a cylinder and clutched them tightly. ''My father never told *me* where to go to school. I guess I should give you the same freedom to make up your mind.''

DeeDee reached across her mother's lap for her father's hand. ''I've always wanted to make you proud of me,'' she said. ''That's why I was afraid to tell you that I didn't get in.''

''You always make us proud,'' Mrs. Smith said.

Mr. Smith nodded in agreement and squeezed DeeDee's hand. ''I guess I did put an awful lot of pressure on you. That wasn't fair. So . . .'' He paused and took a deep breath. ''Wherever you decide to go to school, I'll be behind you one hundred percent.''

''Thanks, Dad,'' DeeDee said.

''And I'm sorry about my—er—accusations the other night,'' he added. ''But you can understand how worried I was when you didn't come home.''

''I do understand,'' DeeDee said. ''But I've always been responsible. You should have given me the benefit of the doubt. You would have trusted Toby, too, if you knew him a little better.''

"I *was* rude to him that night he came to pick you up," Mr. Smith admitted. "I guess I should give the boy another chance. He certainly is a fine basketball player."

Mr. Smith glanced down at the court. The third quarter was starting, and Toby was dribbling the ball toward the Westmoor basket. He leapt into the air and made yet another basket. The Westmoor side of the stadium roared with approval. Mr. Smith, too, waved his Westmoor banner and cheered.

At that moment Toby looked over and caught DeeDee's eye. He gave her a big wave, and DeeDee was thrilled to be singled out by the star of the game. But she was even more excited when her father waved back at Toby and gave him a thumbs-up sign.

Impulsively DeeDee leaned across her mother to give her father a hug. She felt as if a whole world of possibilities had just opened up to her.

"Come on, Brittany!" Martin said impatiently as she hesitated at the entrance to the Pizza Palace after the game.

There was no use fighting it anymore, Brittany realized. Everyone in River Heights thought she and Martin were a couple now, so there was no reason to hide.

Brittany allowed Martin to pull her into

the restaurant. Most of the tables were filled with glum River Heights High students. Toby Jackson had led the Westmoor team to a one-point victory in the last few seconds of the game.

"There's an empty table down at the end," Martin said, leading Brittany past all the hundreds of watchful eyes.

Holding her head high, Brittany forced herself to link her arm through Martin's and smile at him as if he were the greatest guy in the world.

"What kind of pizza do you want?" Martin asked after they'd sat down.

"Do I have a choice?" Brittany asked. "Or do you want to control what I eat as well as everything else about my life?"

"I'm not a monster," Martin said evenly as the waitress came up to their table. "Order anything you want."

"That's what they say to prisoners on death row," Brittany said grimly, but she did order her favorite.

After the pizza came, Brittany took a bite of her slice, but she couldn't swallow it. It wasn't that there was anything wrong with it. There was just something wrong with her whole life. In one week she'd gone from social queen to social outcast. Things couldn't possibly get any worse.

Just then the door to the restaurant flew

open. All heads turned as a tall guy in a navy Talbot blazer filled the doorway. Brittany wanted to fall through the floor.

What was Chip Worthington doing here? Brittany had managed to get away from Martin long enough to tell Chip that she was leaving the game early to go to her mom's shop to work. Chip rarely went to River Heights High hangouts.

Chip stared first at Brittany, then at Martin. The look on his face was hard to read, but it wasn't a happy one.

"Uh-oh," Brittany said, half to herself, half to Martin as Chip marched stiffly toward their table.

"Who's that?" Martin asked, putting down his slice.

"Don't say I didn't warn you," Brittany said, malice creeping into her voice. "I told you I had a jealous boyfriend."

Chip paused in front of Brittany's table. No one in the place had said a word since he'd arrived. Everyone was waiting, breathless, to see what would happen.

"Who is this?" Chip asked Brittany in disgust, pointing to Martin.

"Martin Ives," Martin said boldly, standing to shake Chip's hand.

Brittany had to admire Martin's nerve. He didn't seem afraid at all.

"You tell me who he is," Chip demanded, his eyes glued on Brittany. "What is he to you?"

Brittany tried to ignore the bright, curious eyes all around her. "Gee, Chip," she said lightly, "I didn't know you cared."

"You told me you had to go to work," Chip said, glaring at Brittany. "I don't like being lied to. And how do you think this looks— *me,* Chip Worthington, getting dumped for a geek?"

Martin's face fell as he sat down again, and Brittany couldn't help feeling a tiny bit sorry for Martin.

"Calm down, Chip," Brittany said. "Why don't we all go outside and discuss this privately?"

"Why bother?" Chip said, gesturing to the silent crowd around them.

Suddenly he leaned over, grabbed the front of Martin's sweatshirt, and pulled the skinny boy up out of his chair. *"Nobody* embarrasses me in front of other people," Chip said, "and nobody takes a girl from me until *I* am ready to have her taken."

"How romantic," Brittany said dryly.

"I'm going to break every bone in your body," Chip said to Martin, shaking him.

"Chip!" Brittany pleaded. "Don't hurt him! You don't understand."

Dangling Martin like a rag doll, Chip turned to Brittany. "What don't I understand?"

Brittany was silent. She didn't want Chip to hurt Martin, really, but she didn't want to explain everything in front of the whole school.

"You'd better start talking," Chip said, "or Martin here is going to be flatter than a pizza pie." Chip tightened his grip, squeezing the sweatshirt around Martin's neck. Martin's face began to turn red.

Brittany didn't know what to do. If she kept her mouth shut about why Martin had blackmailed her, then she and Chip were through forever and Martin might be seriously injured. On the other hand, if she told Chip the truth, then everybody, including Nikki and Tim, would know Brittany had tried to sabotage their skit. More than anything, she finally decided, she was sick and tired of Chip's pushing people around.

"Okay!" Brittany shouted at last. "Martin and I aren't really a couple. He *blackmailed* me into going out with him."

Chip's face wrinkled in disgust. "Do you really expect me to believe that?"

"You'd better believe it, because it's the truth," Brittany said. "He saw me steal the spaghetti Nikki was supposed to use in her skit at the talent show, and he said he'd tell the whole school if I didn't act as if I liked him."

All the tables buzzed excitedly. Brittany's face grew hot. She felt like the world's biggest fool.

Chip dropped Martin to the floor in a bony heap. Then he turned to Brittany, his clear green eyes flashing. "You know, Brittany," he said, "I was really beginning to like you. But now I don't believe a word you say. I wouldn't go out with you if you were the last babe on the planet."

He turned his back on Brittany and strode out of the Pizza Palace. Tears welled up in Brittany's eyes. Chip had never come close to admitting he cared about her before.

"Serves her right," Brittany heard someone whisper.

"Brittany—" Martin mumbled, trying to get up off the floor.

"Don't even talk to me!" Brittany exploded. "You totally ruined my life! I hate you, Martin Ives! I hate your guts!"

With tears streaming down her face, Brittany grabbed her coat and ran blindly out of the restaurant.

15 ~~~

"Brittany!" Martin called after her as she stumbled through the parking lot outside the Pizza Palace. "Wait up!"

When would he stop plaguing her? Everyone inside the restaurant knew her dirty secret now. By Monday it would be all over school. So why wouldn't Martin leave her alone?

"Brittany—" Martin began a little out of breath.

Brittany whirled around. "Get away from me!" she cried, her face wet with tears. "You've done enough damage. Now get out of my life!"

"But how are you going to get home?" Martin asked. "I drove you here."

"What do you care how I get home,"

Brittany sobbed, "after the way you humiliated me? You made me look like an idiot in front of the whole school!"

"How do you think you made me feel last year?" Martin asked angrily.

"What did I do to you?" Brittany said.

"You humiliated me in front of everybody in the cafeteria," Martin said.

A dim memory started to surface in Brittany's mind. It had been so unimportant at the time that she'd hardly paid attention. Martin had spoken to her, just once, at lunchtime. Brittany had been surrounded by a huge group of friends, and Martin had come up and asked her out. Well, what did the guy expect? Of course Brittany had said no.

"So I didn't want to go out with you," Brittany said, sniffing. "I didn't have to say yes, you know."

"It was the *way* you turned me down," Martin said hotly. "You laughed in my face and said there was no way on earth you'd ever date a geek."

Brittany bit her lip. Had she really said that?

"I'll never forgive you for it," Martin continued. "I don't think I'll ever get a date until after I graduate."

Brittany stared into Martin's blemished face and remembered how everyone had laughed when she'd turned him down. She had never stopped to consider how Martin would feel.

Brittany shuddered. Martin must have felt like a dirty piece of chewing gum stuck to the bottom of someone's shoe. Brittany knew this because that's how she felt right then.

"I'm sorry, Martin," Brittany said finally. "I didn't realize how much I must have hurt your feelings by what I did last year. I guess I can see why you wanted to get back at me."

For the first time all week Brittany saw a genuine smile on Martin's face. "Thank you," he said quietly. "That's all I wanted to hear."

"What?" Brittany asked, confused. "You mean you tortured me all this time just to hear me say I'm sorry? I could have said two little words and you would have set me free?"

"It wasn't just the words," Martin said. "I wanted to know you really meant it. And I guess I wanted a little revenge, too. I'm sorry I messed things up with your boyfriend, though. He would have eaten me alive if you hadn't spoken up back there."

Brittany fished around in her purse for a tissue and patted her wet cheeks. "You sure did mess things up," she said. "It took me ages to get together with him, and you destroyed it in a week."

"Maybe not," Martin said. "The guy

wouldn't have gotten that jealous if he didn't care about you."

"You think so?" Brittany asked, still sniffling.

"Give him time," Martin said. "Look," he continued, "I don't blame you if you hate my guts, but at least let me drive you home."

Brittany hesitated. "Thanks," she said finally. "It beats taking the bus."

As she and Martin made their way to Martin's beat-up station wagon, Martin asked, "So you're really sorry, huh?"

"I told you I was," Brittany answered, annoyed. "I'll never be that mean to anyone again."

"Even Nikki Masters?" Martin asked. "Are you sorry you almost messed up her skit in the talent show?"

Brittany looked at Martin out of the corner of her eye and blew her nose vigorously. "Don't push it," she said.

As Brittany and Martin were driving out of the crowded Pizza Palace parking lot, Lacey and Tom rode in on Tom's motorcycle.

Lacey paused for a split second before removing her helmet. With its tinted black visor, no one would know who she was. But she'd look awfully stupid wearing a helmet inside the restaurant. She'd have to take it off.

Nervous as she was about running into one

of Rick's friends, especially Calvin, it would be easier just to walk straight in as if it were perfectly natural to be seen with Tom. Maybe people wouldn't think anything of it. Maybe they'd think Lacey and Tom were friends *because* of Rick. But all of this was stupid. Why was she so worried about what people thought?

"Let's order a large pizza with everything on it," Lacey said. "I'm starving!"

The air inside the restaurant was warm and smelled of yeasty dough. The front area by the cash register was filled with River Heights High students. They were buzzing about some big fight. Lacey kept hearing Brittany Tate's name, but she couldn't make sense of the rest.

"Maybe Nikki's here with Tim," Lacey said, pushing through the crowd to get a better view of the dining area. "That way we could sit with them instead of waiting."

Lacey spotted Nikki and Tim sitting at a booth in the center of the restaurant. Robin and Calvin were sitting across from them, their backs to Lacey. Maybe joining Nikki wasn't such a good idea. Lacey started to turn, her mind racing to think of an excuse to get them out of there, but it was too late.

"Lacey!" Nikki called, waving.

Lacey froze. What should she do now? She couldn't ignore Nikki, but she didn't want to call attention to the fact that Tom was with her.

"Come on over!" Nikki waved again.

"Time to face the music," Lacey murmured under her breath. She grabbed Tom's hand. "Let's go," she said.

As Lacey and Tom approached Nikki's table, hand in hand, nobody even looked. Everyone seemed more interested in pizza than in her love life. Lacey allowed herself a small sigh of relief. Maybe she'd overreacted to the whole situation.

"Hi, guys," Lacey said brightly as they reached the booth. "Mind if we join you?"

Nikki smiled and started to scoot over, but before Lacey had let go of Tom's hand, she felt a heavy hand clamp down on her arm.

"Lacey?" The voice was almost a growl.

"Uh-oh," Robin said under her breath. "Get ready for 'The Pizza Palace—Round Two.'"

Lacey turned, her blue eyes widening as they took in the last person she wanted to see at that moment. Rick Stratton was standing there, with Katie Fox by his side. She, too, wore a letter jacket, green and gold, with a swimming logo on the front.

"What are you doing here?" Lacey whispered, her body numb. She was barely aware of the warm pressure of Tom's hand in hers.

"I could ask you the same question," Rick said.

Lacey's mind went numb, too. "I thought you weren't going to the game. Robin said—"

"Robin told me *you* weren't going to the game," Rick said. "But that's beside the point. What are you doing here with Tom?"

"Why don't you ask me?" Tom said, stepping between Lacey and Rick. "And while you're at it, why don't you let go of her arm before I break your fingers?"

"Still acting like the tough guy, huh?" Rick said, roughly pushing Tom's shoulder. "Well, I'll tell you something you might not have figured out yet. I'm *bigger* than you, and I'm *stronger* than you."

"Rick," Katie said, trying to pull him away from Tom, "don't do this. She's not worth it."

"Oh, yeah?" Lacey said, turning angrily to Katie. "What gives *you* the right to judge other people—a girl who sneaks around with someone else's boyfriend?"

"He's *my* boyfriend now," Katie said defiantly.

Robin's dark eyes bounced from Lacey to Tom to Rick to Katie, as if she were watching a four-way Ping-Pong match.

"Don't change the subject," Rick said to

Lacey and Katie. "This is between Tom and me."

"No, it's not," Lacey said to Rick. "This is between you and me, but I don't think we should talk about this standing in the middle of the aisle." Lacey grabbed Rick's arm to steer him away from the table.

"I'm coming with you," Tom said, starting down the aisle after them.

"No, Tom," Lacey said. "I need to do this myself. Just wait for me, okay?"

Lacey led Rick to a quieter back hallway by the pay phone and the rest rooms. "Talk," Rick commanded her.

"I don't like your tone," Lacey said. His rudeness was beginning to bring back all the anger and resentment she'd felt toward him lately.

Rick crossed his arms and waited, his hazel eyes flashing.

"You misunderstood what I was trying to say yesterday," Lacey said. "I don't want to get back together with you. I was trying to tell you that I started going out with Tom a week ago. I know you'll think it's really strange since he's your brother and everything, but it's just a weird coincidence. We never meant for this to happen. . . ."

Rick's lips were pressed together in a thin line, and his nostrils were flared.

"Don't be mad," Lacey said. "There's really no reason for you to be. I mean, you've got Katie now, so it shouldn't bother you if I want to see someone else——"

"Mad?" Rick demanded, his fists clenching and unclenching. "Why should I be mad that my own brother, someone I thought I could trust, has been running around with my girlfriend behind my back?"

"But I'm *not* your girlfriend," Lacey argued. "You said so yourself. I think you're just upset because this was so unexpected."

"My own brother!" Rick muttered. "I can't believe Tom would do this to me! He still thinks I'm the skinny weakling kid that everybody picks on. I'll bet he thinks he can take advantage of me just because he acts like a tough guy. Well, I'll show him who the tough guy is."

Rick pushed past Lacey and headed back toward the main dining room. "Tom!" he bellowed so that everyone could hear.

Tom, still waiting by Nikki's table, faced his brother without fear.

"What are you going to do?" Lacey asked Rick anxiously, following right behind him.

"I'm going to turn myself into an only child, that's what!" Rick yelled as he got closer to Tom. Tom made no effort to run away. He simply took off his leather jacket and laid it on the red laminated table.

"Please don't fight!" Nikki cried, rising from her seat.

"Yeah, come on, Rick," Calvin said. "It's not worth it."

Rick ignored his friends. His face was beet red, and his broad chest was heaving with rage.

"Give me your best shot," Tom said with a grim smile.

"My pleasure," Rick replied, clenching his fists.

"Rick, don't!" Lacey yelled. Desperately she tried to hold Rick back as he raised his fist to strike his brother.

But it was too late.

Rick and Tom have come to blows—will the brotherly battle tear Lacey and her friends apart? Kyle Kirkwood is using his computer to match up couples for the upcoming luau, but Samantha decides to play Cupid when she tampers with the results. Will her scheme to keep her boyfriend backfire? Find out in River Heights #14, *Love and Games*.